MULLIN

A Circuitous Route to America

John E. Mullin

MULLIN
A Circuitous Route to America

Published by JM Studio, 48E 1050N, Chesterton, Indiana 46304.

Copyright © 2020 by John E. Mullin, Chesterton, Indiana.
First Edition.
Printed in the United States of America.
Library of Congress Control Number: 2020905678
ISBN-13: 978-1-7321442-3-1

MULLIN

A Circuitous Route to America

CHAPTER 1

"MULLIN!" a commanding voice boomed down the hill and invaded the small thatch roof cabin occupied by the Mullin family. "MULLIN!" again his voice boomed, rumbling down the hill cutting its way through the cabin window. Mullin's son Edward raced and beat his father to the window and opened the shutter. Both, bleary-eyed and blinded by the bright morning sun, held their hands up to block the sun's rays. A man dressed in black astride a large black horse opened a scroll and begin to read as Mullin and his son Edward peered through the cabin window.

"By decree from Oliver Cromwell, all inhabitants of this northern portion of Ireland shall be moved promptly to England. You shall report two days hence to a ship in Belfast where you will be transported to England. Once there, you will be given a parcel of land to start your new life. I wish you Godspeed." He whirled his horse around and galloped up the slope, with the tall grasses of the hill waving behind him, as if the land was waving a fond farewell. Suddenly the shifting winds grabbed the shutter, slamming it shut, adding to the shock that was already present on their faces.

Oliver Cromwell, who was in charge of England at the time because of the slight age of the heir apparent to the throne, decided that he could corner the market on the woolen trade and fill the English coffers. He planned to do this by using the rich grasses of Northern Ireland to raise sheep; he felt the Scottish were the very best sheepherders. He transferred the Scottish men to Northern Ireland to raise sheep. He felt he needed to move the inhabitants out of Northern Ireland.

The Mullins gathered their things and found their way to Belfast through the cobblestone streets to the wharf in search of a ship that would carry them to England. Landing in Liverpool, they found that there was no land and no money for them or any of the other passengers. They had to make their way on their own.

The ensuing months were arduous times for Mullin as he searched for work to support his family. His older son Charles managed to procure an apprenticeship in a printing company. He would make no money, but it held out a promising future for the boy. Mullin managed to keep his family in a rented room and food on the table by sweeping the streets, hauling trash, and doing odd jobs. After several months, he heard that there were jobs in Alsace-Lorraine. After sending a few letters to a friend, he decided to pack up his family and moved to Alsace-Lorraine. Charles was seventeen and was quite well liked by his employer. He decided to remain in England and become a printer. Edward was just seven years old when his father moved their family to Alsace-Lorraine.

Through a friend, his father was introduced to a Huguenot who already had two ships and was planning at least ten more. He got a job in the shipyards, and Edward went with him and watched him make steel and form it into the needed materials for the ships. Within a short time they moved into a real house. Edward made some great friends over the next two years and had a very happy childhood. One day when Edward was about nine years old he was sitting on a rock alongside the main road leading up the hill to the big houses where the sea captains and Huguenots lived. All of a sudden up the hill came a team of galloping horses, digging in and stirring up the dust. They rounded the curve so fast that the wheels of the cart kicked up dirt on Edward and his friend. It was the captain of the ship that was moored down below in the distance. The Captain was yelling at the top of his voice, "I would sell my ship for a decent navigator." Edward looked at his friend and yelled, "I am a navigator." His friend looked at him and began to laugh so hard that he rolled backwards off of the rock into the grass.

"Ha-Ha-Ha, you don't even know what a navigator is," pointing at him and holding his side because of the laughter. Edward became so angry he climbed off of the rock, walked off towards the town kicking dust back at his friend. "I am a navigator. I am," he talked to himself as he stumbled down the hill toward the town. "I don't care what he says, I am a navigator." He walked into the town till he saw the first man who looked like he was a sailor, and he asked him, "What is a navigator?" "What me boy, that's a tough one. He's the guy who points our ship in the right direction. He uses a sextant." "Where do I get a sextant?" "Well you go down this street to a store with an anchor in the front of it and ask the man inside. But I'm warning ya, it's gonna cost you a lot more than you got."

Edward was a fair-haired, rough-and-tumble boy weighing no more than about four stones. He stumbled his way down the cobblestone street towards the shop. As he arrived at the shop, he noticed in the window a large beautifully polished brass object, the likes of which he had never seen before. He was mesmerized by the lines, levers and the spyglass which was part of its mounting. It shone like the very sun, almost blinding him as he gazed at it, beckoning him into the shop.

A bell rang over his head as he entered the shop. The man behind the counter greeted him with a broad smile, "What can I do you for, son?" "A sextant is what I'd be looking for." The man's smile became even broader, covering almost his entire face. "Well," he says, "you've come to the right place. We sell the most beautiful and accurate sextants in the world. If you buy one, you should buy it here. I must warn you, however, we don't give them away. Have a look at this one in the window. I noticed you looking at it. It's only 800 quid." The shock on Edward's face was evident as the storekeeper began to show him other models. "Perhaps these smaller models would be more to your liking." Edward slowly walked down the counter, looking at one sextant after the other as well as a great array of other items for use on ships. The man leaned over the countertop as his apron draped down and his hand held out toward Edward. He held a small toy sextant, small enough to fit in his hand. "Perhaps this is what you're looking for." It was beautiful, very small, and shined like gold. Edward's eyes filled with delight and sparkled even more than the object they rested on. "How much is that one? Does it work? Can I make it work? Is it real? Does it come with instructions?" "Hold it, hold it, slow down fella. Let me answer one question before you ask another one. Yes it works, probably not the most accurate in the world, but it works. I can let you have it for seven pounds." Edward, of course, didn't have a penny, but he swore he would return one day with the seven pounds and would buy that sextant. The man reached behind the counter and handed Edward a small pamphlet. "These are the directions that will tell you how to use this instrument. Read this over. When you come back you will know how to use it." The pamphlet had a beautiful picture of the sextant on its cover. Edward was mesmerized by it as he made his way out the door down the cobblestone street and up the hill towards home.

When he arrived at his home, a two-story thatched roof stucco structure, he opened the door and ran in yelling, "Ma, Ma, look what I have. Isn't it beautiful?" "Yes, what is it?" "It's a sextant." His mother's demeanor changed rapidly from a smile of joy to an inquisitive frown. "A sex what?" "A sextant, and I'm going to be a navigator. I'm going to be a navigator. Look, look, isn't it beautiful?" She looked at the brochure, smiled and gave it back to him and said, "That's wonderful, but you're going to have supper first." "No, Mama, I mean it. I'm going to be a navigator." She looked again at the brochure and asked, "How much does a thing like that cost?" "Well, only seven pounds. Is that a lot of money?" "Yes, now get ready for supper."

When Edward's father arrived, he showed him the brochure and told him all about the sea captain who said he would give his ship for a decent navigator. His father told him that he would figure out some way for Edward to earn the money he needed. A few weeks went by before his father realized how serious Edward was about earning the money for the sextant. Finally one day his father took him to work with him. It was a very hot summer, and Edward carried water to the workers who were very, very appreciative. He also did cleanup and small jobs around the boatyard as well as fetching materials around the town that were needed in the boatbuilding process. When there wasn't much for Edward to do, he spent time watching his father work. He watched him take iron ore, which he melted in a crucible over a coal fire and poured it into bars, and then he hammered it into hooks, rings and latches, all sorts of things that were needed on a ship.

Over the next three months, Edward was able to save seven pounds. He immediately went to the ship shop and purchased the sextant, which he knew how to operate, because he had memorized every word in the brochure. He got a map of the local area and walked miles and miles out into the hills and waited for dark so that he could pinpoint his location by the stars with his new sextant. He did it so many times that he became very proficient with his little toy sextant.

One day on the occasion of his 9th birthday, many, many ships were in port. Edward loved to walk down the docks to look at the ships. On this particular day he passed by one of the ships and recognized the Captain who had said a year ago on the road that he would give his ship for a decent navigator. He called up to the Captain and said he was a navigator, and he would like a job on his

ship. The Captain laughed and then said to him, "I do need a cabin boy. How old are you?" "How old do I have to be?" The Captain said, "You have to be 10 years old." "I turned 10 today." "You turned 10 today?" "Yup." "Today?" "Yup." The Captain's face grew into a large smile as he looked down at the boy. His trepidation was evident, but he was nevertheless interested in having a cabin boy, especially one who had the guts to come to him and ask for a job. "You have to clear it with your mother. You know that, don't you?" "Oh yes, sure. I would do nothing without talking to my mother first, but I don't want to be a cabin boy. I want to be a navigator." "Well," said the Captain. "First things first. We must first clear it with your mother, and you must first be a cabin boy. You can't just walk into the most important job on the ship without first working your way up to that position. I am willing to take you on as a cabin boy if you want the job." "Oh yes, I want the job. I want the job." "Good," the Captain chuckled. "We will be sailing with the tide next Thursday. Be here with enough clothing to last three months." "I'll be here, don't you worry. I'll be here."

Edward was so excited he ran all the way home. As he approached the house nearly out of breath, he yelled, "Ma, Ma, I got a job. I got a job." His mother opened the door to let him in and inquired, "What kind of a job? How much does it pay?" Edward stopped and tilted his head in an inquisitive angle. "I don't know what it pays. It's a job, so it must pay something." His mother bent down and held both of his shoulders. She inquired, "You have a job, and you don't know what it pays. Do you know what you are to do?" "Of course, I'm going to be a cabin boy for Captain McGregor." His mother leaned in, looked him straight in the face and said, "You're not old enough to be a cabin boy." "Yes I am, Captain McGregor said I was old enough." She looked him straight in the face and said to him, "You didn't lie did you? You remember what your father told you. If you lie, you will burn in the fires of hell for all eternity." She held him tightly and said, "It is a big job to be a cabin boy, and you will be gone for months at a time. You'll be homesick and not able to come home. You'll see land only four days at a time. It's a very hard job. You will need permission from your father." "I will ask him when he gets home."

Less than an hour later, his father came trudging up the road after a hard day's work and was greeted by his son running down the road toward him telling him his story of how he's gotten a job on the ship. Surprisingly, his father was excited about the idea. As he approached his wife, he gave her a wink and a smile. As much as she tried not to, the corner of her mouth turned up slightly. There was great discussion around the kitchen table that night, and the decision was made to have Captain McGregor for dinner the next night to discuss the matter.

The next morning Edward found his way to the ship where he asked Captain McGregor to come to dinner that night. Since Captain McGregor had only had three or four home cooked meals in the past three months, the invitation was happily accepted. Mother Mullin put out a beautiful spread of beef, mashed potatoes and gravy, and peas much to the delight of Captain McGregor. Then she laid out the rules and regulations that Captain McGregor must follow if he wished to have Edward as his cabin boy. "He must learn his numbers. He must learn to read. You must care for him as you know I would, and I expect him back as happy as he is now." Captain McGregor was a strong forthright man who could handle any problem that came his way. He was fair and straight with his men. He would stand for nothing that would put his ship in jeopardy. He was very understanding of Edward's mother's requests, and told her that if it was his son he would ask for nothing less. He would care for him as if he were his own son.

The next morning found the Mullin family standing on the dock, the sun rising over the horizon, while the ship was being readied for sail. The tide began to roll in as the

sails were being hoisted into the sky. The sails snapped
and pitched back and forth against the ropes like a mighty
horse anxious for the start of a race. It was one of the
most beautiful sites Edward had ever seen. The Captain
invited the Mullin family on board to show them Edward's
quarters. As they stepped on deck, the wind snapped the
sails full. The lines to the dock were pulled tight. Mr. and
Mrs. Mullin were quickly ushered off the ship. The dock
lines were undone, and the ship was on its way.

That night was the longest night Edward ever spent
on a ship. The Captain told Edward that this was just a
rolling sea, as the ship climbed over 12 and 15 foot swells.
"Rolling sea," Edward thought as he spent the entire night
with his head between the rungs of the rail, lying there
waiting for the next moment when he could again empty
his insides into the ocean. He was lying there with his face
nearly green when the Captain came and carried him down
to his bunk. It was the only time in his entire career that
he got seasick; he did it all in one night.

The next week it was smooth sailing. Edward
managed to adjust very well. A few months later, he went
to the Captain and was crying. As he sobbed, he said, "I
lied to you, and I don't want to burn in hell so I must tell
you the truth. Today is my birthday, and I am 10 years
old." The Captain leaned back in his chair with laughter in
his voice and said, "Number 1, sailors don't cry. Number
2, never lie to me again. Number 3, do you swear that this
is your birthday today?" Edward looked up as he dried his
tears with the back of his hands. "Yes, today is my
birthday." "Then we must have a party to celebrate your
10th birthday. Go tell the cook I want to see him." The
Captain laid out a great feast with cake made for all hands
during the dinner. He made a toast to Edward Mullin and
told Edward to make a speech. So Edward stood up and

said, "I think I have the greatest job in the world as cabin boy on the ship. If anyone needs anything, let me know, and I will get it for you. I also like my other job as fact checker for the navigator." At this point nearly all of the eyebrows on the ship raised up at least an inch. If you were to total all of the elevations of the eyebrows into one eyebrow, it would have raised as much as 40 inches, except for the eyebrows of the navigator who lowered his eyebrows so much that they could have easily erased at least 20 inches of the raised eyebrows.

Over the next few months everyone on board grew to love and admire Edward. He did his job better, faster, and with more enthusiasm than any other cabin boy they ever had. He loved his job. One day he was in the Captain's quarters. As the Captain was pouring over the maps, he looked up at Edward and said, "Look at this map and tell me where we are, my little navigator."

So Edward looked down at the map and pointed to a spot on the map. "We are here." The Captain looked at him and laughed. "If we were here," pointing to the spot on the map, "I would look out the window and see..." he jumped up quickly and yelled up the stairs as he ran, "HARD A-STARBOARD, HARD A-STARBOARD, HARD A-STARBOARD."

Just then, the ship jolted, and Edward smashed into the wall as the ship rolled up onto a rock and slid down again into the sea as it turned out away from the shore. The Captain was very busy for the next few minutes putting a man out onto a plank so they could look down and see if there was any damage to the outside of the ship. He sent man down below to check to see if there were any leaks and examine the entire ship for damages.

Later, he came back to the cabin and asked Edward how he knew our exact location. Edward told him, "Just before you asked me, I had taken a reading up on the deck. Then I came down, and I was looking over your shoulder at the map. When you asked me, I told you where we were." The Captain was dumbfounded. "You knew exactly where we were with that little toy?" Edward was a little put off by the comment and replied, "Toy! Toy! It is very accurate." The Captain then told Edward, "From now on, you will use the ship's instruments to check the navigator."

The navigator was not too happy about the idea of a 10-year-old boy checking his navigation. But the Captain explained to the navigator that if he did not allow the boy to check his work, he could be hanging from the nearest yardarm. The navigator was an elderly man who had a taste for the rum and spent most of his time in the rum cache. He very seldom appeared to be drunk, because he held his rum fairly well, but his navigational skills were often impaired by this activity. Edward was very careful never to get in the navigator's way or cause him to be

jealous of him in any way. He checked his work after he
was finished and never bothered him while he worked.

Consequently, day-by-day, the Captain's esteem grew
for his young cabin boy. After a time, even the navigator
grew fond of Edward; after all, he had saved his job. A
mistake as large as the one he made could easily have sunk
the ship. He was very lucky that the Captain didn't hold
him accountable. The navigator took Edward under his
wing and taught him everything he knew about navigation.
He taught him how to read all of the charts and locate all
of the ports. After several voyages the navigator was
checking Edward's work. As time went on, their accuracy
became greater and greater. They very seldom missed a
port, which would cause them to go up or down the coast
to find it. Edward began to be recognized and known by
other navigators until he became almost famous because of
his young age and his extraordinary ability.

During the next several years Edward traveled all
around the Mediterranean, the North Sea, and even
around the Horn of Africa. He became the most well
traveled young man on the high seas. One day he saw a
sailor lose his hat to the wind. It flew out on the water and
floated away from the ship at a right angle not with the
wind. Edward put a stick on the end of a long fish line and
put it in the water to study the current, which he drew on
the maps and charts much to the dismay of the Captain
who didn't like those arrows that he put all over the place.
Along with learning his navigational skills, he estimated the
speed of the currents. On several occasions when the skies
were overcast several days in a row, he managed to
navigate and spot their location by watching the currents in
the ocean. He managed to bring the ship in perfect
alignment with one port by simply watching the currents in

the ocean. This amazed his Captain who bragged about it at every port.

Edward became a very strong swimmer. Whenever they were in the doldrums and there wasn't any wind and the ship was sitting still in the water, he would swim around the ship. He loved to swim. He and several other sailors who liked to swim as well swam with him. He challenged them to race him around the ship. He always beat them handily.

One of the deck hands named Jake was talking to the other sailors and told them that he was a very good swimmer. This was the talk of the ship. By the time the ship came to a day of no wind, the entire ship was anxiously awaiting the race, because they all were betting on one or the other racer. The Captain put a rope from the ship to a longboat as a start/finish line. The rules were simple. Edward would start on the outside, and they would race around the bow. When they got to the halfway point, they would switch sides and finish the race. They both hung on to the rope, and the Captain fired his pistol. They swam neck and neck around the bow of the ship and were side by side at the halfway point. At that point, Jake dove under Edward and came up on the other side only losing about a foot. They swam this way around the stern and on the port side toward the rope. Just then, Jake swam as hard as he could and leaped out of the water grabbing for the rope. From the ship it looked like Jake was going to win, but Edward went under, pulled the rope down under Jake, then held it up to show that he won.

One day they came to a port that was on a river, and the current of the river was coming out into the ocean quite strongly because of the showers the night before. The wind was offshore, and the tide was going out. This made it very difficult to impossible to bring the ship into port. The cargo that they had was extremely important. The merchants wanted their materials right away as well as the medicine that was on board for the sick. Edward told the Captain that he would swim ashore pulling a fishing line through the surf against the river current. The Captain would tie a few buoys on a rope line, and Edward would pull them up to the shore and then round up enough men to pull the ship into port. The Captain didn't like the idea because of the danger of swimming against the current so he set out a longboat with several men aboard to attempt to row to shore, but the wind was so strong, it literally blew them back to the ship. Edward insisted, but the Captain would not allow it; it was just too dangerous.

That night Edward and the old navigator tried to accomplish the task. The wind was still strong and swimming in the night was even more difficult. Edward felt he had to try. He swam for over two hours against the current, making his way to the shore. It was totally exhausting as he crawled his way up onto the beach and crossed it in the driving rain towards a light that he saw in a window. He knocked on the door. When it opened, he collapsed into the arms of the housemaid. She took him inside and revived him with some hot cider. He slept for nearly an hour, getting his energy back. The string was still attached to his belt. When he awoke in the early morning just before the sun was to rise, he excitedly told the woman that he had to find men to pull the ship into port. After sunrise the rain had stopped, but the wind was still very strong from shore. Within a few minutes, the man of the house was able to round up ten or more men and began to tug on the fish line. Within a few minutes, they held a fairly large rope. With the help of some horses, they began to pull the ship into the port. Everyone was very, very happy to get the ship into port, because it was carrying medical supplies, which were badly needed to help the town where almost half the population was ill. Edward became a hero for his actions.

At the age of 14, he told the Captain that he had his eye on his job. Again the Captain had a great story to tell everyone about Edward, "Now he has his eye on my job." The Captain spent many hours with Edward teaching him how to sail, how to handle the big rig, how to set small sails, large sails, teaching him the names of all the materials on the ship. He taught him how to handle the winds, storms, when there was no wind at all. He taught everything he knew about sailing and handling men to Edward.

One of the trips, which went through the Mediterranean and up to Venice, prompted the Huguenot's wife to take their daughter to Venice on a shopping trip. The ship was lying in its berth, being outfitted for the trip. Edward was calculating the time so they would catch the tide and began their voyage to Venice. He was talking to the Captain and told him that some of the men felt having women aboard ship was a bad omen, they should not be allowed to be on such a ship. The Captain just laughed and said, "That's an old tale of the sea." The Captain then called all the men on deck and told them that there would be women on board and their language would have to be cleaned up when they encountered the women. They should be as gentlemanly as they could possibly be. Edward told the Captain that he was not fond of the idea of women either. The Captain made him promise to serve the women just as he serves all of the men on board as part of his job as cabin boy. Just then a smartly outfitted horse-drawn carriage drew alongside the ship. A woman and girl were helped out of the carriage. Edward leaned over the rail of the ship, thinking he was not going to be happy at all with women on board, spied for the first time the daughter of the Huguenot. He was 15 years old, just, and she was all of 14 or 15. Edward was dumbstruck. He'd never seen anyone so beautiful. He could not take his eyes off of her. She looked up at the ship and smiled with a beautiful broad smile, like nothing Edward had ever seen before. Edward leaned over the rail to watch her walk up the gangway toward the ship. He leaned farther and farther and farther as she came closer to the ship. Just then a massive great arm grabbed him by the belt and pulled him back in before he fell in the water. Jake, a sailor who was a massive man with muscles bulging out all over his body, said to him, "We call them women. Haven't you ever seen one before?" Edward looked up, pushed himself out of his hands, and said, "Of course, my mother is one of them." They both fell back onto a sack of grain and had a great laugh as he looked up into a blue sky. Edward said, "Have you ever seen anyone so beautiful as the Huguenot's daughter? I can't believe it." "Wait, wait my little man, this could be great trouble for you. Be very careful and stay away from her." Jake advised.

The first night the mother and daughter remained in the cabin, and Edward delivered their food to the door. When he returned to get the tray, he noted that it was barely touched. The second night Edward was told to take food to the cabin, he knocked lightly on the door. It opened slowly. It was the daughter who looked at him, looked down at the steaming hot tray, and threw up all over the tray and all over the front of Edward. She tried to produce a faint smile as she said, "Thank you," and slowly closed the door. Edward stood there in frozen disbelief as he slowly turned trying not to spill anything while making his way to the rail to dispose of the mess on the tray.

The next morning the Huguenot's wife asked that the windows be cleaned on the outside of the cabin. There was a pretty heavy wind that day so all hands were needed at their stations. Consequently, Edward got the job of cleaning the windows. He climbed over the side and positioned himself in a bosun chair outside the window. The windows were very dirty, and he was unable to see anything inside. As he began to clean one side of the window, the other side of the window pushed out quickly, and the Huguenot's daughter put her face through the opening very close to Edward's face. Edward quickly put out both of his hands and pushed himself away from the window as far as he could saying, "No, no." The girl laughed and laughed, saying, "No, I'm not going to throw up." She smiled a big smile and said, "I'm Anna. What's your name?" Edward told her his name. She then went on, "How old are you?" "I'm 15." She hesitated thoughtfully and then said, "I'm 15 too, well almost 15." She sat in the window with her elbow on the window ledge and her chin in her hand watching Edward scrape the window with his blade. "Do you like working on the ship?" Edward hesitated, "Yes but, yes but ..." She smiled even broader saying, "But, but what?" Edward stuttered, "I, I am not supposed to talk to you." She pulled back into the window and started to close it saying, "Okay."

Edward went on scraping the window and began to notice a face on the other side of the glass. She was pressing her nose against the glass, crossing her eyes and wiggling her tongue back and forth. Edward began to laugh. A voice from above, Jake's voice, came down over the rail, "What's so funny about scraping windows?" "Ahh nothing, nothing at all, I was just laughing." He went on scraping the window, and a few minutes later Anna poked her head out again saying, "You missed a spot." Then quickly withdrew her head again and closed the window.

A second later she opened it again stating, "You missed two spots." She again pulled back in and closed the window. Edward ignored her and went on scraping the window. She pushed out the window, put her head out and watched him scrape for a moment. She then inquired, "Aren't you going to talk to me?" Edward turned his eyes to her without moving his head and started to say, "I am." She interrupted, "I'm not supposed to talk to you," wiggling her head back and forth. Edward turned his head and smiled. He then made a gesture with two fingers sliding over his mouth as if he were taping it shut. She gave a kind of grimacing smile as she reached out one hand and acted like she was pulling the tape off of his mouth. Edward laughed out loud again. Again Jake's booming voice came over the rail, "What's so damn funny?" "This job is going to take several days or even more." Jake yelled down, "I'm going to pull you up now. You will have to come back tomorrow." Anna grabbed his foot as he ascended and almost fell out the window saying, "I'll see you tomorrow."

There were windows on two sides of the cabin, all of them needed to be scraped. Edward spent the rest of the evening trying to figure out how he could prolong the time it would take to clean all the windows. He spent the evening hours in his bunk staring at the ceiling picturing her face, her smile, and her nose pressed against the glass. The night seemed as though it was a year.

The next morning Jake lowered Edward over the side, and Anna was sitting in the window with her feet dangling in the wind. "What took you so long?" She inquired. "I came as soon as I could. I had chores to do, and I had to bring you your breakfast." She smiled, "That breakfast was wonderful, and now that I know you brought it, it was even better." Edward smiled and said,

"Thank you, but I didn't make it." "I know," she said, "it was better just knowing that you brought it." Edward swung back and forth in the bosun chair trying to see the window behind Anna. "I am here to clean the windows, but you are in the way." Anna smiled and said, "Well, what shall we do about that?" The wind kept blowing her dress up, and she kept pushing it down while Edward was trying to avert his eyes from looking up her dress while he swung back and forth in the bosun chair. She requested, "Tell me some of the stories of your travels to exotic places. Tell me what you've seen, where you've gone, what you have done in the past five years. Then I will let you scrape the window." Edward began to tell her the stories of his past: the ship sliding off the rock, the blue Mediterranean, sailing around the Horn of Africa, monkeys in Madagascar, Persian rug makers, and so on. Anna was totally captivated and mesmerized by his many escapades.

When Jake came back to pull Edward up, he had yet to touch a window. They had talked all day. When Edward asked her about herself, she said, "This is my first voyage. I'll bet you couldn't tell." Edward laughed out loud, and again the booming voice from above demanded, "It's time to come up laughing boy." Jake began hauling him up while Anna waved goodbye moving just her fingers on one hand. Anna's mother was claustrophobic and spent many hours on the upper deck in a soft chair that the Captain had rigged up for her. Edward always made sure that the mother was on deck before he decided to work on the windows.

The next morning was a beautiful sunny day with a soft breeze from the West that ushered the ship through the Mediterranean blue, a seemingly perfect day. This morning Jake was busy working on the ship so Edward lowered the bosun chair over the side and tied off the rope onto the rail. Then he climbed over the rail, down the side and started sliding down the rope to the chair. When he arrived just above the chair, he looked down. Anna was sitting in the chair. When he saw her, he started to climb back up the rope, but Anna shouted, "No, no, come on down." "How can I?" answered Edward, "You're sitting in the chair." She then pushed her feet hard against the side of the ship and swung out as much as five feet from the ship with Edward twirling around on the rope above her head. "What are you doing?" Edward yelled. She came back towards the ship and pushed off again, this time even farther. Edward was losing his grip and sliding down close to Anna's head. His feet stopped his fall at the knot above the seat. When it swung back closer to the window, Edward jumped in the window and sat on the window ledge, his feet dangling in the breeze. Anna began to swing out and back, and then ran alongside the ship swinging out in a long arc and catching herself with her feet as much as 12 feet on either side of Edward. She was having a grand time laughing under her breath so that her mother would not hear her laughing up on deck. All of a sudden the rope became worn as it was rubbing back and forth up on the rail, and it broke. She dropped into the water. Edward quickly dove in after her knowing that the moving ship could be easily out of sight in minutes if he didn't act quickly. He grabbed Anna and pulled her close to side of the ship. The ship slowly slipped past him, and he had nothing to grab a hold of as hard as he tried grasping at every possible opportunity. When the stern of the ship became equal to them, he quickly swam in and grabbed hold of the rudder, pushing Anna up on the flat space just above the water on top of the rudder. He told Anna to be quiet, and he would throw a rope down to her. Edward then called out as loud as he could to someone on deck saying that he had fallen in the water. Jake threw a rope

down for Edward and pulled him up over the rail. Edward
quickly went down to the cabin just above the rudder,
opened the window and pushed a bosun chair out and
lowered it down to Anna. She sat in the chair, and Edward
pulled her up to the window and inside. "Thank you,

Edward," as her eyes welled up with tears, "you saved my
life." Edward looked very worried, shaking his head no,
saying, "You must never tell anyone about this. This is just
between you and me. If you do, I will lose my job, and
your parents would be very mad." "Don't worry, I will tell
no one. I like knowing something that only you and I
know." As she walked across the room out the door and
into her own cabin, she left a trail of water two feet wide
which Edward immediately began to wipe up all the way to
her door.

The wind was perfect for the next three days. As they rounded the boot of Italy and entered the Adriatic Sea, they landed at Bari to pick up provisions. Within three or four days they would be in Venice. During the next three days Edward didn't see Anna. He was kept busy doing all the jobs that he had neglected while he was scraping the windows. He did not see Anna in all that time. He began to think that she was avoiding him. When they arrived at the port in Venice, he saw Anna on the deck with her mother. When he saw that she saw him, he raised his hand to wave, but she just looked away at her mother ignoring him. Jake was assigned to accompany Anna and her mother around Venice on their shopping tour. As they were walking down the plank onto the dock, Anna said to her mother, "We may need more than one man to carry our bags." "How much are you planning to spend?" her mother retorted. "Well," Anna replied, "not more than you say, but still, I think we should have more than one man with us." Anna's mother looked at her, then looked back at the gangplank. Edward was standing there with the face of a young puppy begging for the last morsel of cake. Her mother looked up at the Captain and Jake and asked, "May we take this boy to carry our bags?" The Captain said to Edward, "Would you like to accompany these ladies on their shopping trip?" Edward turned, saluted the Captain, and assisted the two ladies into a gondola taking a seat in the back with Jake. Jake sat next to him in the backseat looking out of the corner of his eye at Edward every once in a while with a little smirk on his face. Edward looked up at him and began to say something, but Jake spoke first in a whisper, "Be careful."

When they arrived in Venice at the waters edge and walked across St. Mark's Square, the two women were mesmerized by the beauty of the Cathedral, the loggia, bronze horses, rows and rows of columns, and the tallest bell tower they've ever seen. Jake and Edward followed them through the narrow streets, stopping in nearly every shop. They tried on many dresses, hats, gloves, bags, and leather goods--a shopping trip the likes of which Edward could never have imagined. Another shop was filled with glassware, everything imaginable made of glass, from chandeliers to tiny small figurines. Anna was attracted to a glass ball about the size of a cue ball with beautiful colors, blues and greens with some red swirling and churning inside the glass ball. Anna asked if she could have it, but her mother said, "No."

They then went down the street to another store. While they were inside, Edward ran back to the glass shop and bought the glass ball. When Edward got back to the group, he saw Anna modeling a party dress. Edward was awestruck by how beautiful she was in this striking red dress. Anna's mother showed very little interest in the dress, but when Anna looked at Edward, she saw that he liked it. She insisted her mother buy the dress.

The next two days were spent in much the same way, going from shop to shop buying all sorts of different items. Each day when they returned to the ship, Jake and Edward had to solicit help from the other men to carry all the boxes and bags they had purchased. The ship sailed on its return voyage with the cargo that they came to Venice to get as well as all the things that Anna and her mother had purchased. For the next three days Edward did not see Anna, because the two women were playing with all of the items that they had purchased in Venice. When Anna finally emerged from the cabin, she saw a dejected look on Edward's face. When she saw this, she asked Captain Mulroney if she could have the cabin boy give her a tour of the ship. The Captain, a little suspicious but not too concerned, gave his permission and called for Edward.

Edward showed her every square inch of the vessel. But the Captain stopped him when they wanted to climb up to the crow's nest. He said that little girls in dresses should not be climbing over his well-mannered sailors. On their way back to her cabin, she asked Edward, "Where do you sleep?" "Oh, I sleep with the old navigator in his room." She became very interested and requested, "Take me to your room. I want to see your room." "I sleep with old Jim, and he, well he, sleeps a lot, and he's sleeping now." But she insisted, "If he's asleep, he will not hear us. I'll be very quiet."

He was hesitant but gave in. The navigator's cabin was just two doors down from Anna's cabin. Upon entering the cabin, they could hear old Joe snoring. They very quietly walked over to the bunk where Edward slept. Anna jumped into his bunk and rolled around. She grabbed his pillow and started for the door, but Edward grabbed his pillow out of her hand. "I want to sleep on your pillow," she whispered. "No! No! You can't have my pillow." "Why not?" She retorted. "Because, because I need a pillow." "Okay," she said as they slipped quietly out the door. The next night when Edward came to his bed, he found that his pillow was gone. In its place was a lacy, pink flowered pillow. Edward quickly turned the pillowcase inside out so that the lace would not be showing and went to sleep.

The next morning he noted that he had a pair of pants missing. The following night about three bells, Edward had a dream that a horse's tail was brushing him in the face. He kept slapping it away, but the tail kept brushing him in the face. He woke up to discover that Anna was brushing her hair across his face trying to wake him up. "What are you doing here?" he whispered covering himself with the blanket. "You are going to take me to the crow's nest," she insisted. "What! Are you nuts? You sneak into my room in the middle of the night, and you want to go where?" She leaned down close to his face with her hair falling on both sides of his head and whispered, "You are going to take me to the crow's nest." "You can't climb to the crow's nest in a dress." She stood up and said, "I'm not in a dress." "What!" he exclaimed, "What are you wearing?" "I'm wearing pants." "Pants! Where did you get"… He hesitated, "My pants, you have my pants." She laughed out loud, and Edward shushed her saying, "You'll wake up Joe, be quiet." "Come on, let's go, I have never been in a crow's nest, and I want to go now, come on." "Okay," he began to get up, "give me a pair of pants. I know you know where they are." She turned and walked to the drawer where he kept his pants and pulled out a pair and gave them to him. Then she turned her back on him while he got dressed. At the same time Joe stop snoring and snuffled around, while the two of them stood frozen, waiting for him to start snoring again. They walked out on deck to the rail at the bottom of the rope ladder. The warm night air brushed their cheeks as a full moon shown across the almost still water. As luck would have it, Jake had the watch that night. They both knew he would be sure to keep their secret. They climbed the rope ladder, and about halfway up, Edward looked down at Jake. He could see Jake's white teeth smiling in the moonlight. Anna told Edward, "This is so beautiful, it's wonderful. I would like to make this my cabin and spend all the rest of the voyage in my little crow's nest." The moon laid down a sparkling trail of light nearly halfway across the ocean. The flickering light made her eyes sparkle as Edward's unflinching gaze was transfixed on her face. She walked around and around and around the crow's nest looking in every direction. "You can see all the way to the horizon," she exclaimed. "Thank you, I will never forget this night." She gazed up at the millions and millions of stars. "Do you know the names of all of them?" "Well, no, but I love the constellations. That's how we tell where we are in the sea. If you look just there," as he pointed to the Big Dipper, "you take those two stars that make the end of the dipper and draw a line from one to the other and continue it on out to the next star. That star is Polaris, the North Star." As he pointed to the star, he noted that the degree wasn't exactly correct, so he called down to Jake. "Jake, Jake, check your bearing. I think it's off." Jake then looked at the compass and discovered he was off about 3 or 4 degrees. They could feel the ship turned in the crow's nest. "How did you know that?" she inquired. "Well, Polaris was just a little bit, well, it was off. It should've been a little more to the port," he replied. "You are amazing, you could tell by looking up in the sky that we were not going in the right direction," she exclaimed. He looked out to the east and said, "See that," as he pointed to the east. "See what?" she queried. "That," as he pointed even harder, "that almost invisible sliver of light on the horizon." She looked as hard as she could and then she saw the light. "That's the beginning of the dawn. It will be light soon so we better get back. You look really good in pants, but you better not keep them. Your mother might find them, and I would be in trouble." "I will get them back to you, I promise." They made their way back to their cabins just moments before the Captain opened his door and came out on deck.

The next night when Anna went to bed, she noticed a large lump in her pillow. It was very hard. She slid her hand in the pillowcase and moved it around until she found the lump. It was the glass ball that she had admired in Venice. She knew immediately where it came from. She was about to scream with joy, but she was able to catch herself. She smiled so broadly that tears came to her eyes.

The next day they arrived at home port. Edward was so busy that he only managed to catch a glimpse of her climbing into her carriage. They were only in port for three days. Edward visited his parents. On the third day they were back on the sea for another 2-1/2 month voyage. Upon their return, Jake noticed someone on horseback out on a high bluff overlooking the sea. He could tell it was female, but he wasn't sure who it could be. Nevertheless, he called for Edward anyway. Edward came on deck, and when Jake pointed her out, he was sure it was Anna.

Hours later they pulled up to the dock. Anna was sitting on top of a large pile of cotton bales. The second the gangplank was put out on the dock Edward was there looking back at the Captain like a puppy in heat. The Captain smiled and signaled him to go ahead. Edward ran and jumped up to grab her hand. When he hit the bales, they tipped back. They both tumbled down the backside to the ground. They both ended up lying on the dock laughing. Again it was a short stay, only two days this time. He would be away again for another two to three month voyage.

This particular voyage was unlike most of the others, because they encountered a hurricane on the way back. The winds blew strongly across the bowsprit of the ship, pushing them as much as 45° off course in 40-foot swells, many which crashed over the bow. Edward watched in total amazement at the Captain's cool and collected demeanor during such a dangerous storm. He already admired the Captain, but now his admiration grew beyond his own imagination. Edward decided that he wanted to be just like Mulroney. He watched every move he made, how he handled the ship in a storm, all the orders he gave to his men, and was able to save the ship and its crew with his skillful maneuvering through the treacherous waters.

When the storm subsided, the Captain asked their exact location. Old Joe and Edward determined that they were off course by about 100 miles out into the Atlantic. Edward looked at the charts and suggested to the Captain that instead of steering the course straight for the homeport, he should continue at a right angle to that course another ten miles, because according to Edward's chart of currents they would catch a current that would bring them home two or three days sooner. The Captain looked with disbelief at Edward, "You have never been in these waters. How would you know that the current is ten miles from here?" Edward, not knowing quite what to say, responded, "Logic." The Captain looked shocked. "How would you even know a word like that, let alone know what it means." Edward pointed at homeport on the map and stated, "It means we will be in three days sooner." The Captain stood there shaking his head and finally said, "Ten miles?" "In ten or less." The Captain, after a little thought, replied, "We should have a little wager on this." Edward had never wagered before and had some trepidation. At the same time, he felt confident that it had to be very close, maybe 11 or 12 miles he thought. "Let's have a wager." The Captain sailed another ten miles. Edward reported that they were in the current and about to come to the proper compass directions towards homeport. The Captain was still uncertain but definitely felt something under his feet. The Captain, knowing that they were blown off course over 100 miles, thought that they would be back in ten days. They arrived in seven, which surprised the Captain. As they came by the point of land where they spotted the woman on horseback on the last trip, they noticed she was there again. Edward, upon seeing the horsewoman on the bluff, pulled off his shirt, kicked off his shoes and started for the rail when the Captain yelled, "What are you doing?" "I'm going to swim. You won't be needing me, will you?" The Captain replied, "That's a long swim." He jumped up on the rail, looked back over his shoulder and said, "Not for me," as he dove in. About five minutes later Edward climbed the cliffs and mounted the horse behind the lady in red. They disappeared behind the cliff. Jake was at the wheel. He said to the Captain, "That could be trouble." The Captain's eyebrows lowered as he looked at Jake. Jake continued, "If her father were to disapprove, he might even kill him. Unless, of course, it was her father's idea to meet him." The Captain still glaring at him questioned, "And how do you think that would come about?" Jake hesitated for a moment then went on, "Well, let's say some Captain, who has in the past bragged about his cabin boy, would suggest inviting him to one of his dinners, perhaps at the mansion on the hill. He might suggest that Anna might like to get to know him. They're close to the same age, and he is a very promising boy. He could easily be Captain someday. He could be just the person he might be looking for to be a suitor for Anna. After all, she is very close to the age when he would have to find a suitor for her." The Captain's scowl changed to a slight smile as he looked at Jake and replied, "Jake, you are a devious character. You really like that boy, don't you?" Jake shrugged his shoulders and with a sly smile said, "He's one-of-a-kind." "That he is." The Captain turned and headed to the stairs down to his cabin.

Several trips later when Edward was 18 years old, he received an invitation from the Huguenot to attend one of his dinners. Whenever two or three of his ships were in port at the same time, he would have a large dinner at his mansion. This was such an occasion, and Edward was invited. The Captain took Edward to a clothing store and outfitted him with the proper attire. Edward had never been to such a party and had no idea how to dress or act for that matter. The Huguenot sent a carriage to bring them to the party. On the way through the town heading for the large hill where the mansion was, the Captain stopped the carriage in the town square. He entered a candy shop to pick up a small present. He then went down the street to another shop where he picked up some flowers, some of which he gave to Edward to take to the party and present to Anna and her mother.

As they came out of the store, Edward noticed a man hanging from a gallows. He inquired, "Why is that man hanging?" The Captain looked over at the man and said, "He is a navigator." "A navigator?" "Yes." The Captain continued, "He was on one of our ships that was captured by pirates and then later on he was seen with the pirates. He came back here trying to get on another ship. Anna's father hanged him, because he was told that this navigator came back so he could deliver another ship to his pirate friends and become wealthy as well." Edward was in

shock. "Her father can hang people?" The Captain, nodding his head, said to him, "No one can stop him. So let me warn you. Never get on his bad side and never harm his daughter in any way or he will hang you also."

The image of the hanging navigator burned itself into Edward's brain.

The party was a grand success. Edward was able to charm Anna's mother as well as her father. The Captain recounted stories about Edward, including the most recent story regarding the hurricane and his knowing where the current was to get them back three days early. Edward acted very shy and unassuming, not really wanting to take credit for all the bragging that was going on which really impressed Anna's family. Luckily, he made no mistakes at dinner except for one small bobble. He dropped some food on his front, which was quickly removed by one of the servants who was signaled by Anna's father.

At the end of the meal, Anna's father signaled the musicians to play dance music. Edward had never danced in his life and immediately tried to melt into the wall, but Anna's father took her hand and came over to Edward, put her hand in his and said, "This is your dance." Edward was in shock. With his mouth open and his head shaking, he told her father in a quiet tone, "I have never danced before." "Well, Martha, Martha," he called to his wife. "Martha, Eddie has never danced before. Let's take him into the den and teach him a few steps." His wife grabbed him by the hand and pulled him into the room. "Come on, Eddie, I'm a master teacher. I will have you dancing in just a few minutes." Within ten minutes, Edward merged into the ballroom ready to try out his new steps. Anna was dancing with another young man whom she summarily dismissed the minute she saw Edward. Her mother turned him over to Anna and directed the musicians to play Anna's favorite song. Everyone at the party had heard stories about Edward, and they watched in delight to see him trip, bump, and step on Anna's toes. They were all delighted along with Anna's father to see that there was at least

something that this boy genius had a little trouble with.
The evening was an absolute delight. Even Edward, who
was the brunt of much of the fun that evening, was
delighted.

They were on their way back to spend the night on
the ship, which was being loaded and readied to sail with
the morning tide. The Captain spoke to Edward in the
carriage, "You were a smash hit tonight." "I was scared to
death," Edward replied and then said, "Eddie, Eddie,
what's with Eddie?" The Captain laughed right out loud
and answered, "That means he likes you. He has names
for everyone he likes. He calls me Roney. And he likes
you, and you like Anna. You do like Anna, don't you?"
The Captain lowered his head and looked straight into
Edward's face. Edward drew back with a surprised look
on his face and replied, "Yes, yes, of course. Does this
mean that we don't have to hide anymore?" The Captain
sighed in relief, "Yes, you can go right up to the door and
ask her out now. Though, you may have a chaperone from
now on." This turned out to be the case. Every time the
ship came in, Anna would be waiting at the dock in the
carriage with the driver, a footman, and a chaperone. The
chaperone was over six feet tall, 200 pounds, never said a
word, and never left her side any moment that they were
together after that party.

On the next voyage the Captain told Edward, "You
are going to have to learn to dance if you wish to be
accepted in this new lifestyle." Edward then stated, "How
can I learn to dance out here on the ship?" The Captain
looked at him and said, "You are right. Perhaps I will have
to teach you." The next day he was called up to the wheel
deck where the Captain had drawn footsteps on the deck
for Edward to follow so he could learn the steps of the
dance. Edward attempted to follow the steps and found it

difficult with the ship moving up and down and back and
forth in the rolling sea. So the Captain took him by the
hand and began to dance with him. Within a few minutes
the Captain noticed a group of men on the lower deck
laughing at him and Edward dancing. The Captain then
called out each of the names of the sailors and commanded
them to join him on the wheel deck. He then paired them
up and told them to dance with him. After a few minutes
he called out for one of the deck hands who played the
squeezebox to bring his instrument and play for their
dance. Within a few minutes, they were all dancing and
beginning to have a grand time. Edward was finally
getting the hang of it and starting to enjoy dancing as much
as the other men were enjoying it. At this point another of
the Huguenot's ships came up upon them and began to
pass. Most of the hands were on deck watching and
smiling from ear to ear. When the Captain saw this, he
commanded everyone back to their stations. Edward spent
much of the rest of the voyage practicing until he became
quite proficient.

On Edward's 20th birthday the Captain called him
into his cabin, "Edward, it is time." Edward looked at him
inquisitively, "What do you mean?" "I mean," the Captain
hesitated, "I mean Anna's father has decided," he hesitated
some more, "he has decided to have an engagement party."
Edward, with a questioning look on his face, asked again,
"What do you mean?" "Well, Anna's father gave me this
to give to you." The Captain then handed him a small
leather pouch filled with gold coins. "You are to go buy a
diamond ring and put it on Anna's finger. He is building a
new ship, the biggest he has ever built, and he plans to
make you the Captain. He can't have his daughter married
to somebody who's poor." "Married, married, married!"
Edward exclaimed, "I like the sound of it, but I also like
the idea that it should be my idea. I mean...I like to be in

charge of my own life." The Captain leaned back and smiled, "You will have everything you ever wanted, a ship of your own, beautiful wife, and he will probably build you a house on the hill." "Do you think I'm ready for all of this?" Edward questioned. "Of course, you're very young, but you're wise for your age. You handle people very well, and you know everything there is to know about sailing. You have years of experience on the water, and you'll never get lost. I'm sure of that. So I say, sure you can handle it. No problem." Edward had a surprised look on his face. "I'm glad you're sure. I'm not so sure." The Captain leaned back in his chair with both hands behind his head and said, "Just ride the waves and keep going. You'll be just fine. You should be very careful of her old man though. If he doesn't kill you, you will have a great life." He then leaned back in his chair and laughed so hard that he almost fell out of it.

On the next voyage on or about the third day, they spied a pirate ship off in the distance that began to take chase. There was a fog bank in front of them, which normally they would avoid, but in this case the Captain ordered them to go straight into the fog bank. There was little to no wind inside the fog bank. They were sure that the pirate ship would come into the bank at the same place that they had so it was important to move through the fog as quickly as possible. They were ordered to put down the longboats and pull the ship by rowing through the fog. They changed course to avoid capture. The fog was as thick as pea soup, and Edward felt as if he was taking a drink of water with every breath. It was difficult to see the man in front of him let alone know where they were going. Every sound carried through the fog as if it were in an amplifier. The order came to row without making a sound. About 20 minutes into the fog, they could hear clearly the pirates talking to each other. Every noise on the pirate ship could be heard as if it was right beside them. When they heard the pirates say to be quiet, they would stop rowing and wait until they started making noise again before starting to row again. They rowed silently all through the night as the sounds of the pirates became fainter and farther away. At daybreak, some of his men saw that the light was brighter on one side of them so they rowed toward the light. After a time they came out of the fog and found a good breeze which saved their lives. They kept a sharp eye looking for signs of the pirate ship, but there wasn't any sign of them for the remainder of the day. The Captain ordered total darkness that night just to be safe.

The next stop was in Italy near Pisa where the Captain gave Edward the order to go to Florence many miles away to purchase a diamond ring. Anna's father told him to have Eddie buy the ring in Florence. The Captain told Edward privately and quietly to buy a ring with a one karat diamond and then spend the rest of the money getting as many diamonds as he could get. Do not tell anyone about this. Edward rented a horse in Pisa and road to Florence where he was able to get 40 diamonds along with the ring. He then went to the leather market and had a belt made that had a pocket in it where he hid the diamonds and the ring. He spent the afternoon walking around Florence acting as though he was a tourist. He backtracked several times to see if anyone was following him. He ran down several blocks and around corners before he got back to the stable where he left the horse he had rented in Pisa. He changed his hat and coat before leaving town.

On his return home, he went to his parent's home to tell them that he was about to get engaged. He was there only a few seconds when three men came in and put a bag

over his head and dragged him off. They road in a carriage
for a while and then they dragged him into a building and
pulled off the bag. The first person he saw was Anna's
father who reached out his hand and demanded, "You have
my diamonds?" "Yes," Edward replied, "Right here," as
he took off his belt and handed it over to him. "Why?"
Edward started to say, "why?" The old man interrupted,
"I didn't want any of then to perhaps fall out on the floor
at your parent's house." Edward's eyes flashed as he
reached into his pocket and pulled out a coin and slapped
it in the old man's hand. "Here's your change. You don't
trust me, and you want me to marry your daughter?" The
old man was not accustomed to people talking to him like
this, and he felt bad. "Well," he returned, "there is a lot of
value here. I wouldn't blame anyone for being tempted to
take one or two since I didn't know how many you bought.
I would have no way of telling if you kept one or not."
"THAT NEVER ENTERED MY HEAD!" Edward yelled at
the top of his voice. "Maybe we should think this
marriage thing over again." "NO, NO," the old man
insisted. "You're perfect for Anna. She loves you, I'm
sure. I won't mistrust you again, I promise." Edward
looked him straight in the face as sweat came onto his
forehead and said, "If I didn't love Anna so much, I
would…" The old man stopped him and told him, "I will
not mistrust you again. You are a honest person, and I
want you as my son-in-law." Edward started to leave, but
the old man stopped him. As he poured out on the table
40 diamonds and the ring, "How many did you get?" he
asked with astonishment. "40." "40?" the old man was
flabbergasted. "I never got this many before. You must
have driven a hard bargain." "I did," answered Edward.
"I told them because I was buying so many of them, I
should get a quantity discount and not have to pay full
price for each diamond. They went into the other room
and discussed it for a while, then gave me five extra

diamonds." The old man then picked up the ring off the table and held up to the light. "Anna will like this one. You have pretty good taste." He put the ring in Edward's hand and said, "You know what to do with this." "I do, and I will do what you ask with pleasure," Edward answered with a much more pleasant tone.

At the end of the next voyage, three months later, he planned to give her the ring. He practiced many times during the voyage. When they arrived at home port at the end of the next voyage, the carriage was waiting. Edward ran down the gangplank, jumped in the carriage expecting to find Anna waiting inside alone. Anna was there with her mother and the chaperone. All three of them had big smiles on their face waiting to hear Edward's proposal. Edward was completely put off by all the people in the carriage and felt he would wait for a more opportune moment to ask for her hand. The moment never came, because he never found a moment when they were alone.

In two days the ship was readied, and he was off again. During the voyage he talked to Jake about his problem. "They are always with her--the big guy, who says nothing, the footman, the driver, all of them watching every move I make. I'm not asking them to marry me. I want to ask her." Jake, in a sympathetic tone, tried to answer, "Well, you may have to get permission from the old man to have a few moments alone with her. He is a pretty understanding guy if you talk to him right. I'm pretty sure he'll figure out a way." The next time, Edward spoke to the driver first and told him to take him to Anna's father. Edward then talked to her father and explained his situation. The father was very understanding, and said as he pointed to a hilltop across a small valley, "You go home to your parents today, and tomorrow I will set a blanket up there on the hill with champagne, caviar, and a nice lunch. You can be alone."

So it was, the next morning Anna showed up at his parents' front door on a horse with another horse in tow. Of course, a block away there were three or four horsemen following along including Mr. Chaperone. They attempted to be incognito, but there aren't many six foot 300 pound monsters around. They rode to the top of the hill and discovered a blanket fit for a king with everything imaginable including a candelabra. Edward glanced down the hill towards Anna's house, and he could see people in every window looking their direction. He saw a spark-like reflection of the sun off of a spyglass. After eating lunch and having had a very long conversation, Edward got on one knee and produced a ring. Anna jumped in his arms, wrapping her arms around his neck as they kissed. As excited as Edward was at the moment, he could still hear the banging of pots and pans from the kitchen of her father's house and some muffled applause even though it was almost a kilometer away.

The next morning Edward was off again on a short voyage up the coast, which took a little less than a month. Upon his return there were three carriages, an entourage, and even people from the village anxiously awaiting his arrival. He was taken into the village on a shopping trip where they bought an entire new outfit for Edward to wear at the engagement party. Anna and her mother had spent every day of the last month planning the perfect engagement party. They had invited nearly the entire village to attend this joyous occasion. Anna was not a part of this entourage as she was busy with her mother doing the final preparations. The party was to be a sumptuous occasion with musicians, a performance with a small chorus, a huge pig roasted on a spit, friends who came from miles away, and paper bags with candles in them marking both sides of the long lane leading to the main house. Edward was overwhelmed by all the attention.

As Edward's carriage approached the front of the main house, he saw Anna on the front steps. He felt his heart jump in his chest. She was breathtaking in her new gown. Edward became weak in the knees as he exited the carriage and nearly fell down though his eyes never left Anna's eyes. She offered her hand. Together they ascended the stairs into the main room to thunderous applause. Many of the guests were local people who knew Edward as a child and had never been in the mansion on the hill. Edward seemed to be a representative of the common people. One of their own who made it big. During the feast, Anna's father rose and gave a long speech about the many exploits of Edward on the high seas. Included in the stories was Edward's instant dance lesson given by his wife and his consequent toe smashing experience. He expressed his great pride. He felt honored to find such a suitor for his daughter. Then he made a toast to Edward and Anna. As music started and the tables were cleared away, the guests were waiting to see Edward dance. Anna's father announced that the happy couple would dance the first dance. Much to the surprise of the entire party, Edward was able to handle the dancing quite well. As the evening went on, Edward made a pact with Anna that he would come back that same night and climb the tree outside her window so they could be together alone that night.

After the party Edward, along with his mother and father, were taken home in a gleaming black carriage that his father had built as an engagement gift. Upon arrival at their home, Edward told his parents he would be right back and went back out the door. The carriage went down the block, turned around to head back towards the mansion. Edward hid behind a stone wall. As the carriage passed, he jumped on the back where the footman normally stood and road back to the mansion. As he approached the mansion, Edward jumped off and made his way to the tree below Anna's window. He climbed to the top of the tree where the branches were fairly small and tried to swing the tree to get close enough to the window so he could grab it. He swung back and forth several times getting closer each time when all of a sudden the window open, and he saw Anna standing there completely naked. At that moment the tree had snapped. Edward cascaded down, breaking branches and ended up on the ground. Moments later as he opened his eyes from the daze he found himself looking into the face of his favorite 300-pound chaperone. For the first time in all the time that he had known him, he had a smile on his face. Edward opened his mouth to say something, but the chaperone put his finger over his mouth to indicate to Edward to be quiet. He then ushered him to the stable and saddled a horse for Edward to ride home.

The next day Edward went back to the mansion to spend the rest of the day with Anna and her mother and father. He enjoyed the day being waited on hand and foot by the servants and discussing some of the plans for the upcoming wedding. It was decided that a year from then would be the best time to have the wedding. It was a wonderful relaxing day as he sat in the sun and was served by the servants. When Edward left, he looked back at the tree under Anna's window and noticed that all the broken limbs had been carried away, and the tree was trimmed to look as though nothing had ever happened. Edward made a note in his head saying, "I am going to have to thank that fellow the next time I see him."

The next morning as the ship pulled out for another three-month voyage, it passed the boatyard where they laid the keel for the next ship to be built. It was the largest keel Edward had ever seen. He then heard the hammering on an anvil and could see his father hammering away, making all of the steel items needed for the new ship.

On this trip a very sad occasion occurred. Old Joe, the navigator died, and was buried at sea. Edward was so used to having Joe check his work that he was very uneasy that he was the only navigator now, and all responsibility would be on his shoulders. Captain Mulroney was completely confident that he could handle the job and had no fear. It was the first time in Edward's life that someone close had died. It was very traumatic. The only other dead man he had seen was hanging from a gallows in the town square, a memory that was burned in his head.

The year passed rapidly, and the time for the wedding was approaching. All of the plans had been made--the dress, the flowers, the church, every moment planned exactly the way Anna wanted it. Edward was completely decked out in his official uniform. At the appointed time the carriage arrived at Edward's family home and carried him and his parents to the cathedral. At the cathedral he met with his best man Captain Mulroney, Jake, and other crewmembers. They made their way to the front of the church where they awaited the arrival of the bridesmaids and the bride. After what seemed like an eternity to Edward, the bride appeared with her father at the back of the church. The organ sounded as they approach the front of the church. Edward was transfixed at the site of Anna dressed in white, dragging a 15-foot train with two little girls scurrying around keeping the train straight. Edward was so completely dazzled looking at Anna that the rest of the ceremony was just a blur.

After the ceremony everyone was invited back to the mansion where her father had built a ballroom just for the occasion. Anna's father wanted this occasion to be remembered for years to come by everyone who was invited. He had even invited his competitors in the shipping business in an attempt to display his prowess. It was a wonderful party that ran far into the night. Anna's father drank so heavily that he became somewhat obnoxious and loud. He made several boasts and used a couple of them to brag and boast about his ship and shipbuilding. He then got into an argument with his competitors and ended up with a bet of several thousand guineas about whose ship could get to Venice and back the fastest. The situation became so intense that the race was to begin at that very moment. The opponents ran out the door to ready their ships for sailing immediately. Anna's father had the advantage in that one of the ships was loaded and ready to go immediately. As the men began to leave, Anna's father ordered Edward to be the navigator. Edward protested, "I just got married!" The old man recoiled and ordered him again, "You are the best navigator on the sea. I have a lot of money riding on this. I want my best people to carry it off for me. You will go. You will go now." Anna was not present at that moment and was unaware her father had ordered him to go. At this point, her father was in a drunken rage at the thought that someone would protest and began to throw things at Edward and his shipmates to get them to go. He ran out the door after them saying, "There will be great rewards for all of you if you win, and God help you if you don't." Many carriages and horses scrambled and ran headlong down the hill towards the ships. Within minutes sails were raised, and the race was on.

On the fourth day of the voyage Edward spoke to the Captain and told him, "I have been told that pirates have been spotted in the area ahead of us." The Captain told him, "We are in a race, son. We must be first so take us the shortest distance." Following the Captain's orders, he set the course with the shortest distance.

The next morning Edward woke up to a gunshot. Out of nowhere a pirate ship appeared, and the first shot killed the Captain. Moments later, the pirate ship rammed the side of the ship and stormed the ship catching every one off guard. They killed three crewmembers. The pirates then gathered the entire crew on deck and put out a plank. They tied their hands behind their backs. One by one they put them out on the plank, cut their throats and pushed them into the water.

Just as Edward was dragged out of his cabin, he saw one man on the plank turn around pleading with the pirates not to kill him when one of the pirates slashed his head half off with a broadsword. Edward watched him fall into the water and saw the blood billow out across the surface. Edward knew that within seconds the smell of blood in the water would attract every shark for five miles.

CHAPTER 2

"MULLIN, MULLIN, which one of you is Mullin?" was heard from the booming voice of the pirate captain as they lined up the men one by one and pushed each one out onto the plank. There was silence for a moment. Then one of the members who had worked with Edward on another ship stepped forward and said, "I..." Edward stood up and stopped him from saying any more, "I am Mullin." Captain Teague grabbed him by the arm and dragged him into the captain's quarters, "Are these your charts?" Edward replied, "Yes." "Your reputation precedes you. I have heard of you. I am prepared to offer you a chance to be rich. Sign on with me, and you will have a share of the booty." Edward, turning down the offer, replied, "Put the men in the longboats, let them go, and I will be your navigator for one year." "One year! One lousy year! Make it three," the Captain insisted. "One year," Edward insisted. Captain Teague studied him a little longer, then said, "2-1/2 years." Edward replied, "One and one-half years." At that point, Captain Teague lost his temper, jumped out of his chair grabbing Edward by the front of his shirt, lifting him off his feet, and smashing him up against a wall. He pushed his knife in Edward's throat drawing blood from his neck. "Two years, or I will cut your throat right now." Edward, afraid to speak for fear the knife would go further into his throat, shook his head slightly in agreement. Teague threw him on the floor as he left the cabin slamming the door behind him. Edward could hear the muffled sound of the Captain's voice as he ordered his men to put the rest of the sailors in the longboats and push them off.

Edward scurried down into the storeroom and began to throw barrels of food, apples, salted meat, and half empty barrels of water, anything that would float and pushed them out into the water. He grabbed a spar and quickly tied extra canvas around the spar with as much rope as he could find. He then took out of his pocket his toy sextant and nailed it to the spar. He scratched on the spar the compass directions with a note saying five days in that direction and shoved them in the water.

Meanwhile the pirates collected everything on the ship that they could use and transferred it to their ship. Edward hid behind the pillars in the storage room while the pirates plundered everything usable from the room. He then went up on deck and watched the pirates take literally everything they could use from a ship including extra sails, ropes, pulleys, and all of the cargo of goatskins and woolen materials.

Captain Teague ordered Edward aboard his ship just as they pushed off, separating the ships. The men that were left on board began to set fire to the ship and then swung across on ropes back to their ship. Edward, watching from the deck, could see his shipmates in the longboats gathering up the materials that he threw in the water. He could see the bosun finding the sextant that was nailed to the spar.

That evening Captain Teague ordered Edward to have dinner with him and a few of his men. After dinner when they were all sitting around the table drinking, the Captain began to explain to Edward the system that the pirates used. It was a form of democracy. Each man gets an equal share of everything that's taken on the high seas. The Captain, of course, gets two shares. Whenever they fill the ship with stolen goods, they take them to ports of call and sell their booty at which time they divide the money equally among the pirates. Captain Teague once again offered Edward a share saying, "You are one of us now so you deserve a share." Edward answered with, "I am your captive not your partner." Captain Teague replied, "I believe you will change your mind in the future so I will keep a share for you, because I believe once you're accustomed to our ways, you will be happy to take your share."

The Captain and Edward spent many hours talking about navigation, shipping lanes, and what kind of material is being shipped. The Captain became fascinated with Edward's abilities and knowledge of the sea. He showed a very special interest in whatever Edward could tell him about the privateers. This is an encounter, which he did not want to come about. He was very interested to know where they might be and what their firepower might be. Edward knew the plans of his father- in-law's ships that were laid out as much as a year in advance. He hid this knowledge carefully from Teague so he would not encounter their ship that has been his home for almost ten years. Edward knew that his father-in-law sent ships out immediately when they were loaded, most of the time in a two-to-four day turnaround. While the other Huguenots attempted to schedule their departures on the first of the month, this scheduling made it possible to predict where their ships would be on any particular day. By avoiding his father-in-law's ships, he felt he might be able to avoid being seen on the pirate ship, and he felt by not taking a portion of the booty, he would not be considered a pirate.

Edward had made many of his own charts, improving upon the charts that were purchased. Most of the charts that were purchased simply gave a rough estimate of the shape of the coastline leaving out many of the inlets and coves that existed along the shoreline. Edward was very precise in his depictions of the coastlines. These charts became very important to the pirates, because they could hide in a cove that didn't exist on the charts of the ships they would attack. Captain Teague poured over Edward's charts and became extremely interested in the locations of these coves and inlets, particularly the ones that were near the shipping lanes.

After spending several months wandering around the sea looking for ships to scuttle, Captain Teague became more and more interested in the coves on Edward's charts. "Edward," Teague commanded. "Take me to this cove," pointing to a cove on the chart just beyond a point of land around which the ships had to travel. "You have charted the depth of the water in each cove. How did you know the water depths?" "I guessed by the color of the water," Edward replied. "So they are not accurate, just a guess?" Edward directed the ship to one of the larger coves, and they spent two days waiting for a passing ship. On the third day they spotted a ship coming. They raised their sails and came out across the bow of the ship, which would keep them out of sight of a passing ship. The Captain of the passing vessel called out to them, "Ahoy, ahoy there. Are you in trouble? Did you just escape the shoals?" Captain Teague took advantage of the moment and replied through his sounding horn, "We have been stuck for two days, and we just managed to free ourselves." The Captain of the passing vessel, feeling sorry for them having been stuck, called back to them, "Come alongside and have a nice dinner with us before you move on." Captain Teague, signaling his men to stop laughing and be quiet, answered, "We will draw up alongside." The two ships bobbed together slowly through the ocean in a soft wind.

Captain Teague took a few of his men including Edward and went to the other Captain's cabin where they shared a fairly sumptuous dinner. At the end of the dinner the vessel's Captain called for more ale, and within a few minutes he was nearly asleep in his chair. Much to the shock of Edward, Captain Teague got up and walked over to the Captain, drew his sword, and slit his throat while Teague's men quickly slit the throats of two other men who were at the table. Within seconds they were dragged to the window and thrown into the sea. Edward was in total shock. It happened so quickly and so efficiently that there was no way he could possibly have warned anybody of what was going to happen. He was riveted to his seat and began to sweat and shake. He then heard shark fins swirling the water below frightening him even more.

Night had fallen. Captain Teague and his men quietly left the room. Within minutes Edward could hear splashes in the water all around the ship. Edward managed to get up and make his way to the door where he saw Captain Teague signal the men of his ship to come aboard silently and complete the job of disposing of the rest of the crew. Edward watched in horror as Teague's men began to scuttle the ship. They emptied all the stores and put them in their own ship. They took everything of value. Within minutes they had stripped the ship of all materials that would be useful to the pirates and put them in their own ship. Soon thereafter Captain Teague and all the men were back on their own ship. They began to push off when Captain Teague noticed that Edward was still standing on the wheel deck of the other ship. "Edward! Come on, come on!" Edward managed to shake off enough of the shock to run over to the rail and jump across to the parting ship. There were still four or five men on board who were lighting fires down in the hold and several other places. Two of them whisked past Edward as he came aboard, and the others swung across on ropes back to their main ship. They all stood and watched as the ship burned and sank.

As Edward looked at the water that was swirling around with the ship going down, he could see the fins of sharks. Captain Teague put his hand on Edward's shoulder and said, "I think they must follow us, because they are here in just minutes after we scuttle a ship." Several men from the burning ship managed to swim to shore. Edward could hear them talking and calling out to find each other. Captain Teague also heard the voices and called out, "I am Teague, I am Teague." At the sound of Captain Teague's voice, the voices on shore fell silent. Only the sound of falling rocks could be heard as they scrambled up the face of the shoreline running for their lives. Teague then said to Edward, "You will have to find another cove, because they will be watching this one. In the meantime take me to Casablanca, Edward."

Edward set the coordinates for the coast of Africa and Casablanca. Upon their arrival they unloaded all the booty and sold it to the local merchants. That night they set sail for San Sebastian in the Canary Islands. That same evening aboard ship, they all crowded around the bulkhead on the main deck and counted out the money, one share for each man, with two for the Captain.

They spent the next three months basking in the sun and spending nearly all the money that they made. Edward spent most of his time aboard ship. Edward didn't see Captain Teague for nearly a month. Finally one day he came wandering back to the ship where he would spend a couple days and then disappear for a week or two. As the men ran out of money, they would gradually one by one make their way back to the ship. By the end of the third month, they were anxious to get back to sea.

In the meantime Captain Teague had restocked the ship and had it made ready for the next voyage. They departed the Canaries and started up the coast towards Gibraltar where they figured they could see many ships going in and out of the Mediterranean. This was true, but it became a problem when they saw more than one ship at a time. During the ensuing days they saw several ships, but they were all within sight of other ships, which made it very difficult for the pirates to attack for fear of being attacked themselves. They also began to notice that many of these newer ships were carrying more and more cannons. They were beginning to look like warships. They decided to wait farther down the coast to attempt to find a single ship sailing alone.

Edward's charts revealed another inlet farther down the coast that Teague expressed an interest in, so he directed Edward to lead them to this inlet. When they arrived, less than an hour had passed when the signal came from the bluff above that a ship was coming. The Captain set his course to block the passing of the oncoming ship. The ship was a much larger ship and was carrying an entire deck of cannon. Teague gave the order to stay in front of the oncoming ship to prevent the cannon the opportunity to fire. But the oncoming ship made a quick turn to starboard and fired a volley of cannon balls into the port side of the pirate ship. The pirate ship listed to the port side so much that the cannon on the port side could only shoot into the water. The captain of the oncoming ship yelled through his megaphone to give up or his next volley will sink them all. The ship was sinking fast. Captain Teague issued the order to abandon ship. As the pirate ship sank behind them, the men swam towards the large ship. Two of them were shot as they swam toward the large ship. A few of the men began to plead with them saying that they were innocent, and there was no reason for them to be fired upon. The Captain gave the order to allow the men to come aboard as prisoners. Edward seized the opportunity and stayed back thinking he might escape by swimming to shore, which was about 600 yards away. The ship sank to the bottom, but the main mast was sticking out of the water with the crow's nest about 12 feet above the water.

Edward looked around and saw shark fins. He decided to climb into the crow's nest and hide until dawn.

Teague's men swam together toward the ship as their ship sank behind them. The ship's Captain ordered them aboard and began to take them one by one into his office and question them. Edward dived down and swam into the ship, gathered as many charts as he could carry, and swam back up and put them in the crow's nest. It took him three trips to get all of his charts. He swam by two sharks on his way down the third time. He laid the charts out one by one and dried them in the sun.

Teague and the rest of his men sat around the main bulkhead waiting to see what would happen to them. They were surrounded by guards. They were given blankets and later on food. As night fell, the Captain ordered his men to put their prisoners in the hold below. At this point, there were only seven guards watching the prisoners. All of Captain Teague's men had their eyes on him. He was signaling his men only with his eyes, telling each one which man to jump. Then he held up three fingers and put them down again. Then he put one up, then two, then three. At that second all the men jumped up and grabbed all the guards at once. Taking their swords and knives, killing them all almost in an instant. Edward watched from the crow's nest and was shocked and amazed at how quickly and quietly this action took place. They carried the bodies over to a corner by the steps and covered them with sailcloth. Teague then ordered them to go off in small groups in all directions and take care of the rest of the crew quickly and silently. Teague took two men, went to the Captain's quarters, knocked on the door, and waited for it to open. When it opened, out of the blackness through the open door and into the Captain, Teague's sword found its mark. The rest of the night Edward could hear scuffles, fighting, and objects being thrown around.

When the sun came up that morning, Teague had read the Captain's log and told his men to count the bodies. There were ten men still hiding somewhere on this large ship. Teague checked out the large vessel and came to the conclusion that he did not have enough men to operate a ship this size. Just as he was telling his men to try to find the ten men who were still on board so that they could use them in the operation of this large vessel, the voice of a sailor from another ship came over the rail. There was a smaller ship coming alongside that was almost the same as the ship they had just lost. Captain Teague later remarked that his first thought when he saw the ship coming alongside that this is a great Christmas gift. "Is everything all right?" the Captain of the small ship asked. "Why are you not under sail?" Teague answered, "We just sunk a pirate ship. Would you like to come aboard for some tea?" Teague told his men to stop laughing and to put up a curtain of sails. The Captain of the smaller ship said, "We would be happy to come aboard and maybe have something a little stronger than tea." As the men came aboard one by one, Teague sent them behind the curtain. As they went around behind the sail, one pirate slit his throat and two other pirates grabbed him and threw him over the side to the sharks. Once they had disposed of the men who came aboard, the pirates swung over and fought the rest of the men on board. In the end there were seven men left. They found the ten men on the big ship by this time, and Teague took them one by one in to the Captain's quarters and asked each of them to join him. In the end, five of them said yes. As a test, Teague told then to kill the rest, which they did with no problem.

Teague sent a longboat over to get Edward off the crow's nest. Two of the oars were bitten off by sharks on the way over the churning water. Teague told Edward, "Point us north," and they got underway. "Edward," a few days later in the voyage Captain Teague commanded, "take me to Carricacou Island." Edward had collected the maps from all three ships and was unable to find something called Carricacou Island. When he confronted Teague with the dilemma, he put his finger on the map and said, "Right there," twisting his finger around leaving a smudge on the map. Edward set a course that would take them directly to that spot on the map. When asked how long it would take, Edward estimated it would take 2-1/2 months, perhaps a couple days longer.

Much to their amazement, they arrived within days of Edward's estimate. Upon their arrival the men immediately mingled with the natives. Several of them even married them with ceremonies conducted by Captain Teague. After a few days on the island, Edward spoke to Captain Teague, "I promised you I would stay for two years. It is now over two years, and so I am going to leave." Captain Teague was lying in a hammock enjoying one of many perfect days on the shore. He simply looked up at Edward and shook his head saying, "That's true. I still have a share of the booty for you. Would you like it now?" "No, I don't want your dirty money, though I might like to borrow some so that I would at least have some money to get off this island. I will pay you back." Teague, choking back his laughter, pulled from his pocket a pouch full of gold coins, which he handed to Edward, "Consider it a gift since I'm not likely to see you again." Edward went back to the ship, packed up a few provisions, and set out across the island thinking he would find another town and then find his way to freedom.

After two weeks of searching the entire island, he found his way back to where the ship was moored. Upon encountering Teague again he said, "You knew there was no other village on this island! Why didn't you tell me?" Teague choking back his laughter, "You didn't ask. I suppose you'd like to be part of the crew." Edward yelled back, "NO!" "Well," Teague replied, "I could leave you here. Or, I could take you by force." Edward thought for a moment and said, "I've seen this island. I should like to move on." "Well, we will leave again in a month or two. In the meantime make yourself at home, pointing to a cot on the other side of the grass hut that stood on stilts over the still-blue ocean.

Six or seven weeks later there was some unrest among the leaders of the village, and the women were arguing with their men. One of the men was beaten rather severely in his sleep by his woman. He came to the Captain and asked permission to kill her. The Captain got up, grabbed his arm and ordered him to come along as he took him on board the ship. Once on board, he ordered Edward to fire one of the cannons out in the sea. He then waited ten minutes and fired another cannon. All of his hands were on deck in less than an hour. The ship set sail within the next half hour. Some of the men began to question the man who was beaten about what had happened. Captain Teague interrupted them and told them that the man who did this was dead. The sailor smiled even though it was painful to do so. Teague had very strict orders about killing anyone when on leave. Teague told his men that the man was beaten so badly that he would wave the punishment this time.

They sailed down to a new settlement called Clarence Town. They pulled in late in the evening and raided the town taking everything they could carry including pots and pans, sheets and pillowcases, everything from the storehouses. Then traveling up to San Salvador they sold all the goods that they had. Again they divided the money equally with the Captain getting two shares. They spent two months in San Salvador drinking up their money. When they ran out of money or began to cause too much trouble in the town, they shipped out again. They always found the ship well stocked and ready for a voyage, because the Captain always used his second share to ready the ship for a quick departure.

They went on north again to a fairly new settlement, Arthur's Town. They fired one volley into the waterfront, and the townspeople abandoned the town running for their lives. Teague's men ransacked the town once again, taking every salable item, and then sailed over to Nassau where again they sold everything and divided up the money. There was never any doubt that Captain Teague was in charge. On many occasions the Captain would sit down with his men and together they would make decisions as to where to go and what to do next. Teague would often lay out his plans for the future, and the men would vote whether or not they wanted to follow his plan. There were never any attempts at mutiny or efforts to go against what the Captain wanted. Edward felt that this was because not one of them would have the wherewithal to handle a ship or the men that ran it. Though the Captain was cruel when dispensing punishment, he was fair in all other dealings and held the opinions of his men in high esteem. Edward wondered how he could hate and revere this man all at the same time.

During the months that they spent in Nassau, Edward spent much time trying to find someone on the island who could help him escape. He found a man who said he could book passage for him on a ship that was due to come in the next few months. He was a short, humped-over, oily, weasel of a bloke. While talking with him, Edward found out that there was a price on Captain Teague's and his navigator's head. He wanted to make a deal with Edward to split the reward money. All Edward would have to do would be to point out the two men: the Captain and the navigator. Edward wanted to know why the navigator had a price on his head. This oily shrimp of a man told him that the navigator was a traitor and was worth almost as much as Teague. The oily man knew from some of the other pirates that the ship in the harbor was a pirate ship.

He wanted to know the identity of the two top men on the wanted list. Edward was shocked to find out that information about pirates travels faster than they do. When he asked this oily man how he knew this information, he was told that in the past few months there have been two privateers in the port asking questions as to the whereabouts of pirates. Privateers were commissioned by the ship-owners and given ships to go out and clear the oceans of pirates. Some of the privateers became pirates themselves operating under the flags of their nations and blaming many of their robbing and killing on the premise they were chasing pirates. Edward reported this information to Captain Teague much to his dismay and disgust. He felt it necessary to avoid the privateers, because they were larger, faster and had more guns. Teague was very interested in knowing how soon the next ship was coming in and asked Edward to go back to the oily man and find out more information about the incoming ship. Ed went back to the oily man and gleaned more information from him, telling him that the ship in the harbor was not a pirate ship. He told him he was interested in booking passage on the ship coming in and wanted to know what it was carrying, because he wanted to know what kind of accommodations he could expect to have on board. The oily man said it was a cargo ship and that it should be in a month or two. Teague decided it would be a good ship to scuttle, and they should meet it as it came close to Nassau.

Two weeks later he ordered the ship out of the harbor into the open ocean where they waited for the incoming ship. About a week later the ship was spied on the horizon. As it approached, they identified it as a privateer, not a cargo ship. Teague gave the order to move out of the way, hoping that they would not notice this movement as running away but simply another ship moving out of the harbor. The privateer fired a volley, which splashed in the water less than 20 feet from the ship. He ordered, "More sail, more sail," and the chase was on. They sailed north with the privateers right behind them, gaining on them by the minute.

When night fell, he ordered course changes hoping to disappear by morning. It was a clear night, and the moon betrayed them. Their maneuvers didn't gain much larger space between the two ships. The following day the privateers closed the gap again, and again they fired a volley, which came very close while still falling short of its target. Again he changed directions, and again late in the evening, the moon betrayed them. They managed to increase the distance by quite a lot, but they could still be seen on the horizon by the privateers, who mounted even more sail in an attempt to catch up. They sailed as fast as they possibly could for the entire day, losing only a small amount of space between ships. The next night was much more accommodating as again they changed directions, heading across wind hoping to increase their speed. In the morning there was no sign of the privateers, which was a relief for all of the crew. Teague gave the order to continue to sail as fast as possible away from the area.

Two days had passed with no sign of the privateers when they came upon a smaller ship headed for the Americas. Teague gave the order to come alongside and scuttle the ship. It was a smaller ship without any protection, a hopeless situation. All on board were thrown in the sea and the cargo stolen. Edward advised the Captain not to burn the ship for fear that the smoke might reveal their position, but it was too late. The crew was trained to burn the ships they scuttled. The flames and smoke were already rising high in the sky. What seemed like only moments, later the call from the crow's nest came, "PRIVATEERS!" The chase was on again with more weight on board and more draft in the water. The ship was slower, causing the privateers to gain on them at a quicker rate. Though they were still miles away, it was evident that they were gaining. When night fell, it was dark, no moon. Catching a good solid wind, they moved as rapidly as possible with full sail at a right angle from the original course. They headed straight for land, hoping that this move would throw them off. Edward and Teague poured over the charts trying to craft a strategy that would save their lives, when three of the men came in the cabin and told Teague that one of the new men was plotting with four of the other men to mutiny. Teague demanded the name of the mutineer. "Murphy," quickly came from the three men. "Is that the guy with the nip in his ear?" Teague demanded. "Yes," they all replied. Teague then reached in his pocket and pulled out a leather pouch like the one that he had given Edward back on the island, and tossed it on the table. "The first man that brings me his ear, the one with the nip in it, will get this purse," Teague instructed. The three men raced each other out the door, and their quick footsteps disappeared in the silent still of the night. Moments later the sound of a heavy splash in the water was heard in the cabin. Three men returned and knocked on the door. As they approached the table, Teague demanded, "You got the ear?" "Yes, sir," they replied as one of the men dropped it on the table. Then the men requested that the money be divided three ways as they all had a hand in the deed. He opened the pouch and made three equal piles of coins. As he did so, he looked at Edward and asked, "Are you sure you don't want this money, Edward?" Edward looked at him with a scowl and said, "I don't want that money." Teague pointed at the money saying, "This was on Edward, guys. Thank you." Teague then took the ear out on the deck and nailed it to the main mast, as a reminder to everyone not to try anything like that on his ship.

While he was gone, Edward had devised a very risky but bold plan to get the privateers off of their backs. The plan was to go behind the barrier islands along the coast of America and across a very narrow and shallow sandbar at the north end of these islands. The chart showed the depth to be only six feet. Their ship drew eight feet. Teague was very skeptical at first when Edward explained his plan. He asked, "If we would go aground and can't get off of the sandbar, what is Plan B?" Edward answered, "Simple, we abandon ship and disappear into the jungle." Teague stared into Edward's eyes a very long moment and then said, "Let's do it."

Over the next two days the wind off of the land shifted and changed many times during the day causing the privateers to come close enough to fire their cannon. One cannonball smashed through the back of the ship, and three others put holes in the main sail. The men scrambled to change the sails and mend the larger sails as it turned in behind the islands and started up the narrow waterway between the land and the islands. As they entered the waterway, the order came to shove their cannon off the ship with the hope that it would clog the channel as well as making the ship lighter so it would only draw their normal seven feet. As he approached the end of the channel and the sandbar between them in the open sea, Teague ordered the men into the two longboats with the hopes of making the ship even lighter. With ropes attached to the boats into the front of the ship, they would be able to row and pulled the ship over the sandbar. There were many variables. The sandbar could be shallower. The charts could be wrong. The wind could be too weak. They could be sunk before they arrived. All the men, even Edward, were in the longboats rowing as fast as they could to get ahead of the ship and pull it across the sandbar. The ship was under full sail with only the Captain on board and everyone pulling as hard and as fast as they possibly could as they approached the sandbar. As the Captain turned the ship into the sandbar, the wind off the land shifted and gave him an extra boost. The ship slid up onto the sandbar as the wind pushed the sails. The men pulled as hard as they could on the oars as the ship slowed, scraped against sand, then held steady for about 100 feet when it began to slow almost to a stop. Everyone put their backs into the oars as hard as they could possibly pull. Two oars snapped from the great pressure. Teague heard the sound of Edward's voice, "Barnacles." Barnacles were the one calculation that was missing from the plan--barnacles. For months the ship had been collecting barnacles on its bottom, which slowed the ship tremendously. Some of them could be as thick as six inches on the bottom of the ship. They managed to keep the ship moving across the sandbar to a point where more than half of the ship made it across but about ten feet of the ship was still sitting on the sandbar when it stopped. The waves were coming in from the ocean pushing the ship up and back with every wave as the men pulled and tugged on their oars to free the ship. The privateers were coming closer and closer until once again they were within cannon range. The ship had to turn to go over the sandbar. This enabled the privateers to turn so the side of their ship faced the pirate ship. The guns on the side of the ship were much larger. The men continued to pull as hard as they could, fighting the waves and trying to pull the ship off of the sandbar. Everyone heard the order to fire from the captain of the privateers. All 12 cannons fired almost simultaneously. Three of the balls struck the stern of the pirate ship, tearing off a large portion of one corner. Several other balls barely missed the longboats, making large splashes and almost sinking the boats. The cannonballs that struck the back of the ship moved the ship forward at least five feet, almost pushing it off of the sand. The next three waves rocked the boat and lifted the stern just enough so the men could pull the ship off the sand. At this point the ship, being in full sail with a strong wind at the back, made it very difficult for the men to grab onto the ship and make their way on board. One of the longboats swirled around, knocked three men off and filled with water. Then it was dragged by the ship out to sea leaving the men behind. The rest of the men from the second boat were able to climb on board with much difficulty and lower some of the sails so that once again they would have control of the vessel. They cut loose the longboat so that they could go and retrieve the men in the water. The enormous blast from the broadside caused the privateers' vessel to move sideways and go aground a few hundred yards short of the sandbar. The privateers' ship was much larger than the pirate ship. It had a draft as much as 10 to 12 feet which made it impossible to cross the sandbar.

That night under a stiff southern breeze Captain Teague and his men celebrated their great fortune. They traveled on up the coast northward to a small settlement called St. Augustine where they sold their goods. They spent the next few months repairing the ship. He also managed to buy two small cannons to replace the ones that were jettisoned. During their stay at St. Augustine the people became very nervous and mistrusting of them. The town had been ransacked several times by other pirates so they were very suspicious of the fact that this ship had such grave damage and were asking questions as to why, without getting many answers. Teague became very upset with the attitude of the locals and made the decision to ransack the village just before leaving. They looted and burned most of the buildings on Main Street. All of the villagers fled leaving everything in the village sitting in the open waiting to be taken. This prompted the men to dub the village Easy Pickens. They went along the coastline and came to a place called Charleston, a very small settlement that had great need for supplies. They sold their supplies that they had taken from St. Augustine. The people were very grateful to receive supplies and told them about larger settlements farther north that were well supplied from England and France. Teague was intrigued by this information and decided to go north along the coast to see what could be found.

Over the next few months they ransacked several small settlements along the coastline. When they arrived at Cape Charles, the ship was loaded with all the silver and gold they had stolen along the way. It was time once again to sell the booty. After spending a few days in a place called Hampton, Edward suggested that it would be a good idea to sail up river to get the ship out of the sea water and into the freshwater which would loosen the barnacles, enabling them to be able to scrape them off. The next two days were spent searching for a place to scrape barnacles. They found a place where the tidewaters were high enough to bring the ship in, and when the tide went out, the ship would settle on the bottom. By pulling on the topmast the men could heel the ship over enough so that they could scrape off the barnacles. The freshwater made it very easy to remove the barnacles.

It was now almost three years since Edward became a captive of the pirates. He seized this opportunity to escape. He volunteered to be one of the rope pullers, which meant he would have to go out and tie the rope to a tree. Edward told the guys with him he was going to go into the woods to relieve himself. He then disappeared in the woods. The Captain was watching as Edward went into the woods and ordered several men to follow. Edward could hear the men cracking and breaking limbs as they came into the woods so he began to run.

CHAPTER 3

"MULLIN, MULLIN," shouted the men who were sent to follow him. He came to a hill, climbed up on top, and knelt behind a large rock. He then peeked over to see where the men were. He saw them running in the wrong direction back towards the ship. He thought that it was very strange. He then looked at the rock and noticed his shadow seemed to be much larger than it should be. There was a shadow of what looked like a feather sticking out of the top of his head. Edward very slowly turned his head and looked behind him to see a large dark red man standing over him with the sun at his back. They both

stood and looked at each other for a moment. Then
Edward began to look to one side and the other for a way
to escape. At this point the Indian grabbed him and threw
him facedown on the dirt, tied his hands behind him, put a
leather strap around his neck and began to push and shove
him deeper into the woods.

It seemed to Edward that they had walked for several
hours when they came to a smoke-filled village of grass-
covered huts. He was forced to his knees in front of an
old, leather faced man with deep-set eyes and a very large
nose. The man spoke in a tongue that was unfamiliar to
Edward and began to point to a few old women across the
way. Edward was then dragged to these old ladies who
were barely more than half his size. They communicated
with him by using long sharp sticks, constantly poking him
and jabbering as they drew back to poking again. The old

women used him to do all of their chores: washing the gourds and bowls, collecting wood, building fires, sweeping up, all the while choking him with a strap around his neck and poking him with the sticks. That night they tied him to a stake and fed him by throwing bones at him that had pieces of meat on them. He had to fight the dogs off if he wanted to eat. Edward thought about escaping, but nearly every night the wolves came and cleaned up the scraps around the village. Several nights during the next month the dogs woke the village when the wolves came too close. Edward was poked awake twice a night and made to build up the fire to keep the wolves away. One night the wolves got one of the dogs, dragging it off in the woods. Another night while the oldest woman came out of her hut to poke him, she walked off into the woods and never returned. Edward wasn't sure if he was happy or sad for this old lady. She had poked him for the last time.

Several months passed, and the nights became colder and colder. Edward began to wonder if he would make it through the winter. Then one day a small band of Indians who were dressed completely different from these Indians came into the village. They sat down with the chief and traded several items. After sharing some meat and corn, they got up to leave. The men walked over to Edward and untied him from the stake, grabbed the leather thong around his neck and pulled him along with them. The old women who had poked and prodded Edward the past few months were yelling and waving their arms at the old chief who paid no attention to them whatsoever as Edward was taken in tow off through the forest. It was a three-day hike deep into the interior. Edward was afraid he would never see his beloved ocean again.

During that trek they climbed over several high ridges and down along several rivers until they arrived at a pristine village located in a wide valley with a winding stream running through its center. There were forests and high mountains in the distance. A perfect setting with 20 or so teepees had smoke drifting slowly into the clear assure sky. This group of Indians was much cleaner, happier, and had much more respect for their fellow man.

Edward was given his own teepee to live in. He had to share with most of the dogs in the community. Though he was no longer tied, he was watched every day and made to do the same chores that he did in last village.

Every morning he would go out and pick up sticks in different parts of the forest, which were used to maintain the fires. At night he was not watched by any of the Indians. He was told to stay in the teepee, which he did. If he even put his head out of the door, the dogs would go crazy. The Indians would come to make sure he didn't escape. Over time he became more and more trusted. One of the younger Indians who was assigned to watch him became his friend. Edward learned sign language as well the spoken language from this young Indian. His name was Menaucook. Edward, in turn, taught Menaucook to speak English. As the winter came on, it was more and more difficult to find wood.

One day as Edward and Menaucook were searching the mountainside for firewood, Edward stepped on a rock that slipped out from under his foot and cascaded down the hillside exposing a black rock underneath. As Edward examined the black rock, he discovered it was coal. Back in the village there was much discussion, and scouts were sent out to find new sites for the village because of the lack of firewood that could sustain them through the winter. Many of the villagers liked this location but were beginning to give into the notion of moving. Edward convinced Menaucook to help him carry these dirty black rocks back to the village. Menaucook was afraid that they would be ostracized when they got back to the village for carrying black rocks along with very little firewood. When they arrived back at the village, Edward put on a demonstration in front of the chief elders in the large meeting area where he set fire to the coal. For the first time he spoke in their native tongue, poorly at first, but still made himself understood as he explained to them the value of coal. He showed them that it burned hotter and longer than wood. He explained that they would have to use much less of it to achieve the same amount of heat.

He designed and constructed some litters that could be carried by two men, one on each end with a woven basket in between that could be loaded with coal. One trip to the mountain would bring enough coal to last two weeks in all of the tepees. What's more, it would burn through the night, and you would not wake up cold and have to rebuild a fire in the middle of the night. Since the game in the area was still plentiful, the decision was made to winter in the same location. Edward was one of the litter men for the next few weeks. Later younger men took over the job.

As Menaucook was being put through the training to become a warrior, he was held in great favor because of his work with Edward. Edward by this time was becoming very proficient in their language as well as sign language. As Menaucook was taken on hunting trips and scouting trips, Edward was allowed to go along. On one of these expeditions Edward discovered a mountainside covered with red rust. Once again, he told his Indian friends he wanted to carry rocks back to the village. The hunters found it very amusing, and they laughed at him on the way back as he struggled carrying these red rocks. Menaucook was not as skeptical as his friends and helped carry some of the rocks. Edward remembered how his father created slabs of iron that he forged in the coal. When they got back to the village, Edward fashioned a crude bellows out of two pieces of bark and leather. He fashioned a forge out of a pile of rocks with the bellows blowing air up through the rocks to the coal burning on top causing it to achieve the temperature needed to liquefy the iron ore. He put the ore on a broken piece of pottery and put it on the coals. The ore melted into the shape of an icicle about 5 inches long, heavy on one end and pointed on the other, much to the amazement of his Indian friends. This icicle shape was very crude and rough, but it convinced Edward it would be possible to create even better iron by creating a hotter fire. He remembered that his father used coke to create the hotter fire. The Indians thought he was crazy when he wanted to collect their urine to pour on the burning coal to turn it into coke, which would create a hotter fire. He was able to make enough coke to continue his experiments, but the winter came on quickly with as much as two to three feet of snow which made it impossible to continue. It was an extremely harsh winter with strong winds and blowing snow.

Edward was revered and honored during the winter in the big tent. The Chief thanked Edward for finding and teaching them how to keep warm with the fire rocks.

During the ceremony the Chief gave him the name Firestone and a headband with an eagle feather. This was a true right of passage and acceptance into the tribe. After the ceremony, there was much celebration in spite of the cold winter outside. There was a great feast of venison, corn and berries saved from the summer. After they ate, the Chief introduced his daughter to Edward. She was stout with scraggly hair, many teeth missing from the upper jaw, a very large nose that leaked profusely. Her scent was that of a dead skunk. The Chief said though she

was not good looking, she had a kind heart and would make a wonderful mate for anyone who would be inclined. Edward tried to be as diplomatic as possible, knowing that he should not offend in any way a man who could hold his fate in his hand.

The winter dragged on, but Edward was quite comfortable in his teepee with seven dogs. With the risk of smelling like the eighth dog, he rigged up a crude bathtub out of hides and bathed the seven dogs with lime soap that he made from the ashes from the fire pits. The rest of the winter was spent mostly in survival mode. With every day getting shorter and shorter and colder and colder, he spent many hours picking fleas off of the dogs and teaching them tricks such as sit up, rollover, speak, fetch, jump over each other, and attack. It took all winter, but he got rid of all the fleas. The dogs were very happy and began to follow him everywhere he went except at night.

One night he got up to relieve himself. The dogs went crazy, barking, jumping around and waking the village. They remembered their training to warn everyone if Edward went out of the tepee. Whenever Edward did something in the village, he would find the chief's daughter beside him anticipating his every move and helping him in everything he was doing. He tried hard to avoid her at all times, but she seemed to be everywhere. He began to study her and see if there was anything he could do to make her bearable, short of putting her in the lime dog bath. He couldn't think of anything that could possibly improve her appearance. He finally inquired as to what had happened to her and found out that she had fallen off a high cliff and landed on her face, knocking out her teeth and breaking her nose. Later when he related the story, he said, "The only thing that saved her was the fact that she had landed on a dead skunk."

The winter was an extremely harsh one. At times there was four to five feet of snow, making it almost impossible to get out to find food. The winds blew up to 50 miles an hour for three days in a row. Many of the Indians didn't come out of their tepees for many days. Edward went on a hunting trip that took over five days before they killed enough game to feed the whole tribe. Whenever there was a break in the weather, Edward and Menaucook spent much of their time climbing up the mountain to a high rock face overhang that overlooked the village. It was a picturesque spot that allowed a view of the entire valley below. They spent many hours sitting up

there talking and just enjoying the view. Edward had
never been in such a place before with so many friendly
peaceful people. They seemed to love every day and
everyone around them. They reached out to help their
neighbors just as they had helped him when he was in
trouble. He watched as they passed each other and treated
each other as family. They thanked the animals they killed
for giving up their lives so they could live. They used
every part of the animals. Nothing ever went to waste.
Even the bones were used as decorations, toys, tools as
well as food for the dogs. When they accepted him into
the tribe, he was treated as one of them. His skin color
made no difference.

As the winter drew to a close and the snow began to
melt away, the village became more and more active. They
began to prepare for a festival that would express their
thanks for making it through the winter without the usual
losses of people from the tribe. Edward was told that most
winters claimed at least four people, and this winter hadn't
claimed even one. The Chief proclaimed that Edward's
fire rocks saved his people from this dangerous winter.
The winter gave into spring, the spring to summer, and
Edward was having so much fun as part of the hunting
parties as well as a gatherer, that he forgot all about his
attempting to make steel out of local materials. The Chief,
however, did not forget. It was about midsummer when
the Chief called Edward to his tepee. He held in his hand
the icicle shaped piece of pot metal that Edward had
created the summer before. He asked him if he could
create more of this material, because it was the hardest
material he had ever encountered. The Chief had
sharpened the end of the icicle on a stone, which the
women of the village used to poke holes in the skins that
they had dried. The other end of the icicle shaped pot
metal was used as a hammer as well as a pistol to powder

corn and wheat. They had found many uses for Edward's icicle, and the Chief was finding it difficult to allocate its use to all who wanted to use it. Edward began rebuilding his crude forge. The winter had been very unkind to the bellows that he created the summer before, so he found it necessary to create a new one. He and Menaucook set out for the mountains to find the rusty rockslide that provided the materials the summer before that he had made the icicle with. The Chief's daughter followed him around like a lost puppy. She never talked to him and stayed behind him about ten to fifteen feet. On many occasions he tried to lose her or go out from the village without her behind him but was only successful on a few occasions. On this occasion she picked up many rocks in a basket on her head and followed him back to his forge. She carried twice as much as both he and Menaucook carried together. She stayed back far enough that she was often not even noticed by Edward except when the wind was behind them and her stench attacked his nose. It was unbearable to Edward, and even Menaucook got to a point where he did not want to go with him when he left the village. She never went with them when they went up to the mountain because of her fear of falling again. It was a warm summer. He felt that he should move on to try and find his own people, but the people of the village were so loving and kind to him that he was torn between leaving and staying. The Chief was a very wise man and noticed Edward's unrest. On one occasion he told him that if he left he would understand. He told the Chief about the sea, how much he loved to sail and how much he missed being out on the moving waves. The Chief told him, while grabbing a hand full of dirt and pouring it out of his hand, "I like land that doesn't move under my feet." Edward spent many evenings talking to the Chief about many subjects. The Chief had a great interest in how people around the world lived, their dress, homes, making steel, his father, etc. His interest was

insatiable. Every question led to another one and on and
on. Several times during their conversations he would yell
out, "MOVE" and the smell wafting through the tent wall
would subside. The Chief was a very wise man and talked
to Edward on many occasions about the history of his
people and how to understand and handle his people. He
taught him respect for the land and the animals that kept
them alive. He questioned many times the existence of
one God when there were so many different things that
happen in nature and in life that would be very difficult for
only one God to handle. He expressed how difficult it was
for him, as a chief, to think for all of his people at once.
The thought of only one God was difficult to understand.

When food became short, hunting parties were put
together to go out and replenish the much-needed meat.
The hunting parties began to avoid asking Edward to go
with them because of what they called his smelly tail.
Edward talked to the Chief about this problem, and he
took care of it by forbidding his daughter to follow
hunting parties. Edward once again was asked to be a part
of the hunting parties. On one of the hunting parties they
were quite successful. By the second day they have enough
meat to go back to the village. As was the custom, they
built fires, which they kept burning all night to keep any
predators away. On this night they hadn't built a fire big
enough to last the entire night. Late that night the fire had
gone out. They awakened suddenly to the growls and
snarls of a mountain lion that was eating their game. One
of the Indians jumped up screaming and running towards
the mountain lion. The lion turned and in one swift slash
of his paw clipped the Indian in the leg throwing him five
or six feet through the air. Edward and the other Indians
fired six arrows into the night towards the sound of the
cat. They could hear the rustling on the forest floor and
the sound of a carcass being dragged through the woods.

Quickly, two men picked up the carcass meat and carried it up the creek bank back towards the camp. When all of a sudden out of the brush came the mountain lion, hissing, growling, and striking with his paws at the carcass, which the Indians held between them and the lion. Despite the fact that the mountain lion had three arrows in his side, he acted as though nothing was wrong. Within moments Edward and Menaucook had put four more arrows in the lion. Though the lion was still striking, Menaucook jumped on the lion's back, stabbing him several times with his knife. Edward estimated that it weighed 350 pounds or more as they drag it up to their camp. The rest of the day was spent traveling back to the village. Upon arrival at the village, they were treated as heroes because, though they had seen many mountain lions, no one had ever killed one. The Indian with the slashes on his leg was considered the greatest hero. The next few days were spent telling the story of the killing of the lion. Edward began to notice that each time the story was told the lion became fiercer and the battle more dangerous. Edward overheard one of the children telling his mother about the lion battle, saying that the Indian with the scars on his leg from the lion fought for half an hour before finally killing him with his knife. The Chief finally ordered the hunting party into his tent and asks for the truth about the incident. The Indian with the bandages told him exactly how it happened. Even though he had exaggerated and extended his part in the killing, he told the truth to the Chief. The Chief looked to Edward and nodded. Edward nodded back assuring the Chief that the story was true. Later in conversations with the Chief, Edward asked why he didn't tell the truth to his fellow tribesmen. His answer was, "His wounds will hurt less if they are marks of valor, than if they were marks of error."

On another of the trips they were hunting in the high country far south of the village. They hadn't seen any game for several days, when they spotted a 10-point buck standing on the top of a ridge. It was quite a long shot so they decided that all four of them would shoot at the same time hoping that at least one arrow would get him. One arrow hit the side of the buck, two fell short, and another went over his back.

With such a long shot, one arrow could never bring down an animal that size. But he fell on the spot. There was a large hollow between them and the deer and many deep rocks and crags below so it was necessary to walk around the ridge to the other side where the deer lay. When they finally arrived, they found two arrows on the other side of the deer. So they began to look around to discover where these arrows came from. On a ridge about 100 feet on the other side of a deeper drop off they could see Indians, one with an arrow in his shoulder. The other Indians were holding him and taking the arrow out. They walked around this deep hole and found their way through the woods to the place where the Indians were dressing the wound. As they broke through the woods, intending to help them, they were met by flying arrows, one of which hit one of the members of their party. They grabbed their fallen comrade and carried him deep into the woods where they discovered he was dead. They buried him under a pile of rocks. They waited and watched the carcass of the deer to see if the other Indians would come to claim it. They waited through the night without a fire, but the other Indians did not return. The next morning they collected the carcass and carried it back to their camp, where they prepared for the trip back to the village. Upon arrival at the village they related the story to the Chief. The Chief knew the tribe by the arrows that were in the buck. He sent out an envoy with a peace offering to give to the other Indian tribe. The envoy was to find the other tribe and present them with the peace offering so that there would not be a war. Weeks went by, but the envoy did not return.

One morning Edward and Menaucook climbed the mountain to the overlook to watch the sunrise. As the sun rose and the long shadows shortened, they noticed Indians off in the distance, sneaking through the woods, staying in the shadows, and moving quickly from tree to tree. They thought of shouting a warning, but the wind was against them, and it was too far away for anything to be heard. They decided to run back to the village as quickly as possible and warn the villagers. They climbed down to the valley floor as fast as they could. They picked up large sticks on the way and ran into the village to fight the Indian raiders. Just then an arrow came straight at Edward. Menaucook jumped in front of Edward and blocked the oncoming arrow with his forearm, deflecting it away from Edward. He didn't see a second arrow coming and it hit him in the chest killing him instantly. Edward caught him as he fell and put him down on the ground. At that moment everything went black. The next thing he remembered was opening his eyes and seeing his feet being dragged through the dust on the ground and then seeing beaded moccasins close to his face as he was dropped in front of another Indian. Edward noted, out of the corner of his eye, an Indian holding straps that were around the necks of four dogs. When he saw this, he yelled, "ATTACK," then pointed to the Indian who had him by the hair. The dogs immediately broke away and charged. They bit the Indian, who was holding Edward's hair, in several places and went for his throat. The Indian let go of his hair. Edward ran off through the woods keeping himself behind trees to stay out of the line of sight as he ran. He could hear the war hoop of the Indians and the screams of the women and then the yelps of the dogs. These sounds grew more and more faint as he got farther away until he could only hear the sound of his footsteps and his hard breathing. His heart was racing as he climbed the rough trail that led to the lookout.

He made his way up the mountain to the high ridge where he could see the entire village and the valley below. By this time the Indians had killed almost everyone in the village and were looting their homes. They were taking everything that might be useful. Smoke was rising from every tepee. There were many screams from the women as they were being herded together and dragged from their tepees. As far as he could see, all the men of his beloved village were dead. As he watched, the vast amount of smoke swirling around in the wind obscured much of his view. He could see, however, one of the Indians running up to the man with the beaded moccasins, who was dressing his wombs from the dogs. He presented him with an object. Edward could not quite tell what it was, but when he held it up to the light he could see that it was the pot metal icicle. As he watched them converse with each other, he noted the use of sign language that meant paleface. Then after a few more words he pointed at the ground and then along the path that Edward had taken in his rush to leave the village. The Indian in the sparkly moccasins called three of his warriors, pointed at the tracks on the ground and then in the direction Edward had taken. The three warriors then walked with their heads down and followed Edward's tracks. Though Edward's head was still spinning, throbbing, and aching like nothing he had ever experienced before, he knew that he had to press on or be killed. He decided to climb up over the peak of a high ridge. Edward had been this way before with Menaucook and knew that there was a sheer cliff on the other side. They climbed down to a narrow ledge, which was located about ten feet above the top of the evergreens below. These evergreens were over 100 feet tall. Menaucook had dared Edward to jump to the treetops, but they decided it was too dangerous. If they did, it might take two days to get back to the village, because they would have to walk all the way around the mountain. Edward reached the top, slid down the rock face to the ledge. He then walked the ledge, which became narrower and narrower until he was directly over the evergreens below. Edward said a small prayer, crossed himself and then jumped. The treetops were about ten feet out and ten feet down from the ledge. The small branches at the top could not possibly support him. He went crashing through the small branches breaking as many as 20 before reaching branches that were strong enough to support his weight. The wind was whistling through the branches, and the treetops swayed back and forth under his weight as he scrambled to move down through the many branches. He found it necessary

on several occasions to move away from the trunk as much
as five feet in order to snake his way through the many
branches. Down and down he went as the branches grew
larger and larger. He came to a point where he was
standing on the lowest branch. It was 50 feet above the
ground. There was a sheer rock face about four feet away
from the tree trunk. The tree had very large crumbly bark.
He attempted to straddle the tree and hang on to the bark,
but it ripped away in his fingers. He nearly fell. He
decided to put his feet against the cliff, his back against the
tree and slowly walk, sliding his back down the tree.
About 25 feet down, the space became narrower until it
was only two feet, making it necessary to change positions
to continue his descent. In doing so, he grabbed a piece of
bark to pull himself around. The bark gave way and broke
off sending him tumbling toward the ground. He landed
on his back on a bed of pine needles that were as soft as a
feather bed. There were over three feet of needles that
have been piling up there for a hundred years. After a few
moments lying in the needles, his adrenaline rush began to
subside, and he told himself that he must get back to the
problem at hand. He gathered himself together. He began
to climb down over rocky areas and through very thick
trees, down and down, over 400 feet to the valley floor.
Once he was down on the bottom he could hear the
babbling of a brook. He was extremely thirsty and hot;
the brook was a welcome sight.

He began to follow the brook down the valley as fast
as he could move through the untouched land. Though he
felt that he should move as quickly as possible, he could
not help but notice how pristine this valley was. He came
upon many animals, none of which had any fear of his
presence. In fact, they seemed not to notice him at all. At
one point he saw many fish in the stream so he searched
for a stick and found one with three prongs on the end.

He sharpened these prongs and went back to where he saw the fish. The fish seemed to pay no attention to him as he slowly entered the water and put the three-pronged stick close to them. He then jabbed as quickly as possible and got one of the fish, which he devoured within minutes abating his hunger. He thought that this land would have been a veritable paradise for the tribe that he had just left behind.

As the shadows grew longer and the inevitability of nightfall looming, he began to look for some shelter for the night. He saw a small overhang of solid rock with a dark area underneath of soft dirt. It was about 20 feet up, a rise that would afford him the ability to see a greater distance. He walked in the woods and collected many fallen branches and sticks, which he carried up to this overhang. He proceeded to create a wall of sticks in front of the opening, pushing them in the ground and wedging them against the stone above. Once the wall was finished he dug out an area in the soft dirt to sleep in for the night. Several times during the night he was awakened by grunts and noises just outside his stick wall. It was too dark to determine exactly what they were, but several of them were very large animals. At one point he was awakened by something rubbing on his sticks.

He caught a glimpse of a campfire. Edward speculated that they must be a few miles behind him, probably near the bottom of the tree that he had descended. He thought the Indians following him must have been celebrating a successful descent of the tree. As he tried to catch another glimpse of the fire, he began to think about what had happened in the village. An overwhelming sorrow came over him as tears ran down his face. He wondered what might have happened to the Chief's daughter, thinking that she must have been killed because of her maladies. At this thought his sorrow grew, but then he thought, *if I am feeling this way for her, I must have had some feelings for her?* He thought again…. *NO, NO, that's not possible…not possible.* Just then he heard a sniffing noise along the bottom of his stick wall as day was beginning to break; he could see there was a skunk sniffing between each stick and finally blowing the smell out of his nose, almost a sneeze, then slowly sauntering away making all sorts of grunting and squeaking noises as though he were talking to himself. This prompted Edward to smell his armpits and thought, *I must smell pretty bad for a skunk to dispel my scent from his nostrils in such a manner.*

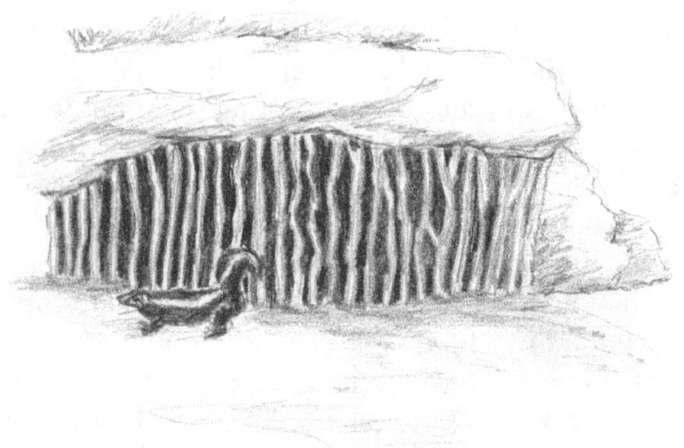

Edward abandoned his cave and continued to follow the stream. At one point a butterfly landed on his shoulder and moved his wings, opening and closing them very slowly. He put his finger under the butterfly, and he stepped on. Then Edward spoke to him saying, "I would love to stay in your valley, but I cannot." The butterfly flew in a big circle and then disappeared into the woods, as if to say, "Okay, goodbye."

The sun shone brightly through the thick forest canopy forming many spotlights of color shimmering on the brook. As he followed the brook, it became a stream, six to ten feet wide. The cliffs on either side narrowed and came closer and closer to the stream until there were sheer cliffs on either side of the water about ten feet wide. Edward waded in the water, which ran one to two feet deep, when he heard the noise ahead of falling water. When he arrived at the falls, he could see that it was about ten feet down to sheer rock below. His first thought was to jump into the water below, but he had no idea how deep the water was. Knowing that any injury could lead to his demise, he turned and went back upstream to the forest where he had remembered seeing several long grapevines hanging from the trees. He climbed up one of the trees and pulled loose the many clinging branches of the vine and held onto the tree limbs. After pulling the vine branches loose from the tree and letting them fall to the ground, he went down, found a sharp edged rock, and chopped off the bottom of the vine. He now had about 25 feet of vine with a loop that he had fashioned with the upper branches. He then floated downstream. When he came to the falls, he laid the loop over a large outcropping and descended the falls as water pounded on his head and shoulders. He reached the bottom instead of the slippery rocks with the water pounding on his feet. He lifted, shook, turned, and yanked on the vine till it freed itself and fell in the water behind him. He then walked in water for another 200 yards to another falls, which was about 20 feet high, and again there were sheer rock faces on both sides of the falls going up over 100 feet. He hung his vine over the falls as he had done before and shimmied down to the bottom. He loosened the vine in the same manner as before then continued downstream only to find another falls. This one was much higher than the other two, and the vine did not reach the bottom. There were some rocks jutting out on the side that he felt he could perhaps swing to when he reached the end of the vine. He felt that this was the last falls, because it opened out onto a very wide lush green valley floor. He hung his vine at the edge of the waterfall and slowly made his way down to its end. He then attempted to swing back and forth and finally made his way to a rocky ledge 12 feet or so above the bottom. He swung back and forth several times, but his attempts were thwarted each time, because he swung out into the waterfall causing his hands to slide down and making it necessary to scramble back up for fear of falling off the end. He decided that if he could swing out then under the water through the falls, then push off with his feet against the wall next to the falls, he would then swing out far enough to make it to the ledge. He pulled himself over to the side away from the falls. By pulling on small cracks in the wall he managed to get himself five or six feet away from the falls. At this point he bent his knees and put his feet against the wall pushing off as hard as he could in a long arc swinging into the falls. As he smashed through the falling water, the pressure was too great causing his hands to slip. He fell the remaining 12 feet into the pool of water at the bottom. He swam across to a sandy beach on the other side and fell asleep.

When he awoke, he was dry and had no idea how long he had slept. In a panic he got up and began running along the bank of the stream until he was almost exhausted. His hope was, if he followed the stream it would lead to a river, and a river would lead to a settlement, since most settlements were built at the mouth of and along rivers. He then thought that his pursuers would think the same thing and would be able to catch up with him knowing where he was going. With this thought in mind he decided to take to the woods to lead them away from the water. He then walked for several hours through the woods and not worrying about giving his trail away, thinking that later he would make his way back to the stream and lose his pursuers. He then heard in the distance something that sounded like a waterfall. It grew louder and louder as he approached. He then heard laughter and large water splashes. He crept closer and discovered that he had gone around in a circle and was back at the waterfall that he had just come from. The Indians who were following him were climbing up the rocks, jumping over to the vine that he had left behind, then climbing it to the top and jumping into the water as they laughed. They were having a great time. Edward lay in the weeds about 200 yards away and observed the Indians having their fun.

After about 20 minutes, he watched them cut a deer into quarters, which enabled them to carry it. Two of the Indians strapped the deer quarters to their backs, said goodbye to the third Indian, and went off through the woods in the opposite direction from his position. The lone Indian packed up a few pieces of meat, which they had cooked over a fire, and began searching for Edward's tracks that led him downstream away from the pool. They had left behind several large chunks of meat and bones that they were unable to carry. Edward, realizing he had at least three hours before the Indian caught up, decided to take advantage of the leftover meat. Some of the coals were still warm, and he was able to start a small fire and cook some of the meat. He was extremely careful not to disturb anything, because he knew that the Indian, after following his trail, would return to the same spot. He did not want him to realize that some of the meat was gone so he carefully tore pieces of meat off of the bottom without disturbing the position of any of the meat. In less than an hour he had cooked enough meat to eat and to carry with him. He was careful to put out the fire in the same manner as the Indians.

Then he walked downstream, carefully stepping in the same footprints the Indian had left behind. He did this until the trail turned into the woods. At this point he jumped over the weeds on the bank and into the water. The stream was about 12 feet wide and ran one to two feet deep. He was very careful trying not to leave any trace of his footsteps on the bottom. He stayed in the stream for at least half a mile until it became three to four feet deep making it difficult to move as quickly as he felt he should. He looked for rocks on the side to use to climb out of the river in order to leave no trace of his exiting the stream. He was then very careful trying to leave no trace of his footsteps behind. As he reached the other side of the valley, he came to high ridges and mountains where the stream began to snake its way over, under, and around many boulders and rocks. It became difficult to impossible to walk alongside of the river. He then came across a log that was hollow. He rolled the log into the water and climbed inside thinking he could maneuver through the rapids and make good time down the river. As he climbed in, the water rushed in the other end and nearly drowned him inside the log. The log was about five feet long and could hold him, but the water rushing in the front, over him and out the back, was unacceptable. He discovered that if he would let his legs hang out the back and put his weight on the back end that the front of the log would rise above the water. He could still see ahead and prevent water from coming in. This enabled him to steer and make his way through the rocky overhangs by moving his feet from side to side like a rudder. Using this method he was able to manipulate through the rushing water, dodging rocks and boulders, keeping himself in the fast water. The river began to widen into a landscape on both sides. There were dense forests on both sides of the river. He could see outcroppings of rocks through the trees. He had been in the forest before when night came and knew how dark it could become. Clouds were rolling in over the mountaintops and darkness was coming on rapidly. He made his way a few hundred yards to the cliffs looking for a place that might have an overhang, which might protect him from the rain. He found what he was looking for, a dry sandy bed that looked as though it had been there for centuries. He hollowed out a flat spot where he could rest and eat some of his meat.

The rain poured for several hours during the night with frightening thunderclaps, several of them very close, knocking down a few trees. The swirling wind sprinkled him during the night. As frightening as the rain and storm was, he felt that it would help him cover his tracks, making it difficult for his Indian pursuer to follow. In the morning the rain was subsiding, and Edward felt he should keep moving as quickly as possible. Since he had such great success with his log, he went back, rolled it back in the water, and continued downstream. About every hundred feet or so, there were rapids. With the rain of the night before making the stream flow more rapidly, it was an exciting ride that took him very quickly over several miles downstream. As he moved down the stream, boulders became larger and more difficult to maneuver causing him to bang from one side to the other until finally he was knocked out of the log. He maneuvered his way through the rapid moving water, around rocks and over boulders finally making his way to the side where he was able to get out. He had several bumps and bruises, but nothing was broken.

He then made his way over the rocky side of the river, which was much wider, now nearly 30 feet across. After about half a mile the rapids were behind him. The river was wide and flat. There was a flat area about 40 feet wide between the river and the high bluffs. He decided to climb one of the bluffs to see if he could see over the trees. Perhaps he would see some smoke or some sign of civilization. He reached the top of the high rocky peak. He looked over all of the trees. It was a stunning view; he could see for miles. The clouds parted, and the sun warmed the rock. After being cold all night and in the water all morning, it was a welcome moment to revive himself on the rock, dry out, and try to plan his next move.

He laid there for over an hour. When he set up and looked downstream, he saw the Indian coming back upstream searching the shore for signs of Edward's tracks. He found them and began to follow them. Edward immediately searched his surroundings and discovered that there were three ridges in a row with low valleys between. He decided to descend and ascend the next ridge, then ascend the next ridge, which had an entirely rocky top. On the third ridge he ran on the rocks as far as he could until the ridge began to go down. At this point he was far out of sight, so he descended and ascended again the ridges he had just come over making his way back to the river. When he reached the river, he found a limb about 20 feet long with two short limbs sticking up. He pushed it in the water and swam, pushing the limb as fast as he could swim into more rapids and faster water. He laid on the long straight limb hanging onto the two short branches which he used to steer the front of the limb while he dragged his feet behind in an attempt to control his ride.

The log bumped and crashed against the rocks below causing him to lose the meat he was saving. He felt thankful that the two stubby limbs were there, because his hands would be banging against the bottom if he had to hang on to the log without them. As he bumped and twisted through the strong current, he felt confident that he was putting a good distance between him and his

pursuer. The river was so swift that he almost lost the log
on several occasions.

After an hour or so he came into another slow spot in
the river where he pulled over to the side to rest and dry
out. Moments later he heard footsteps far in the distance
of someone running through the underbrush. When he
peeked up over the riverbank, he could see the Indian
running. He ducked down quickly and found a hiding
place nearby under a tree whose roots had been washed
out by the river. He quickly crouched beneath the roots
and waited to hear him run past. He could hear very
heavy panting as the Indian stopped behind a tree. Then
he heard him make his way over to the cliff wall about 40
feet behind the tree and sit down. A few minutes later all
was quiet, and Edward thought that he might have left.
He slowly, making no sound, peeked up over the roots to
see if he had gone. The Indian was leaning against the wall
with his eyes shut. Edward ducked back down under the
large root system and waited. Moments later a squirrel

walked down the roots to investigate Edward's presence. The squirrel looked at him through the roots trying to see in the darkness below the roots, squeaking and chattering as he darted his head back and forth. Edward was afraid that he would wake the Indian and reveal his position. He slowly pulled out his sharpened stick and moved very slowly towards the squirrel. Just as he was ready to strike, an arrow pierced through the body of the squirrel and into the tree root. Edward tucked himself back as far as he could under the roots. The Indian came and took the squirrel back to his spot by the cliff wall.

Edward then heard the Indian gathering fallen twigs and sticks, which on two occasions brought him very close to discovering Edward's hiding place. The Indian built a fire. Very soon the nice aroma of the squirrel being cooked over the open fire made Edward hungrier and hungrier as he smelled the meat cooking. Just then he heard the squealing of a pig about 50 yards back upstream. Then he heard footsteps running towards the sound. Edward quickly climbed out from underneath the root system, climbed up over the top of it, looked around the tree to see the Indian still running the other way. Edward ran over to the fire grabbed the stick with the squirrel meat on it and ran downstream as fast as he could. He ran about a quarter-mile, jumped in the water and swam across to the other side. He ran another quarter-mile and went back across the river, all the while taking bites out of the meat. He continued doing this for several hours until he was almost completely exhausted.

When he decided it was safe to rest for a moment, he sat on the bank of the river in some tall weeds so as not to be detected. As he sat, he noticed across the river a chair with three legs. The corner with the missing leg was resting on a stump that had been chopped with a hatchet. When he saw this, he immediately swam across the river, which was about 60 feet wide at this point and quite deep. He climbed out of the river by the chair and looked for a trail. He found one that was quite narrow at this point but grew wider as he followed the trail. As he ran, he looked over his shoulder many times and thought that he saw his pursuer hot on his trail. This made him run even faster down the trail, which led to an open field where he saw a small vegetable garden. He looked back and again thought that he saw some flashes of light from something moving behind him. Edward was afraid he would be caught in the open field so he skirted around the edge until he found a hole in the ground under some berry bushes. He dove headlong into the hole and hid, trying his very best to breathe silently, which he found extremely difficult to do after running in such a panic for so long. His heart pounded against the earth so strongly that he was afraid it would reveal his hiding place clear across the field. He pushed himself as deeply into the hole as he possibly could fearing his feet might still be visible. He tucked them up as tightly as he could. Just then, two extremely strong hands grasped his feet yanking him out of the hole and dragging him out onto the grass.

Edward rolled over and looked up at a large head silhouetted in the sun. The color red filled his eyes, as two strong hands grabbed his arms and lifted him to his feet.

He took a long deep breath, which he planned to use to scream for his life, when he saw the face of the man holding his arms. He looked into a large, red freckled face with a flaming red beard. "What's your name, boy?" the large red haired man inquired. "How did you get here?" Edward, coming down from his adrenaline rush, tried to speak, but found himself having to swallow a few times to bring himself back to his senses. He was covered in mud and dirt from having been in the river and then in the hole. "I am Mullin, Edward Mullin." Just then a female voice from one end of the open field inquired, "Who is that?"

CHAPTER 4

"MULLIN, MULLIN," the large man yelled back at the woman. Edward then looked back across the field and saw the Indian standing beside a tree. The Indian held up his open hand about shoulder high. Edward did the same. The big man, seeing this, turned to look where Edward was looking only to see that nothing was there.

As he walked across the field, the large red haired man introduced himself, "McNally, James McNally," as he extended his hand. Edward offered his hand, and they walk together across the field past the garden towards his wife, who was introduced as Sarah. They both acted a little leery at first, probably due to his appearance and smell, and the strange circumstances that brought them together. They took Edward into their home, allowed him time to clean up, gave him fresh clothes, and set before him a sumptuous meal. They asked many questions. Edward gave only short answers as he tried to keep himself awake. McNally had several horses in a barn with one empty stall where he set up a bit of straw for Edward. Edward bundled up in a horse blanket on the straw and slept through the night, the next day, as well as the following night. Sarah, fearing he might be dead, sent her husband out to check on him in the morning. "Mullin," his voice forced its way into Edward's slumber. He opened his eyes to see the same red face he had seen the day before. Chills of fear went through him as he remembered the circumstances of the day before. "You have slept for over 40 hours," McNally's large strong voice pierced the shadowy stall. "You must be hungry by now; breakfast will be ready in a few minutes. When you're dressed and ready, come up to the house. We'll have breakfast ready."

Edward pulled himself together, got the sleep dust out of his eyes, then made his way to the house. Breakfast was set for five: James, Sarah, Jimmy, a 14-year-old boy, Amy, their 7-year-old daughter, and Edward. Flapjacks, sausage, milk, syrup, things he hadn't seen for over five years or more. Edward told them he couldn't thank them enough, not only for the food, but also for saving his life. Then he told them the ordeal he had just come through to finally end up here. Sarah was worried about Indians being so close, but Edward assured her that these Indians came from far away and would probably not be returning.

Edward spent the next few days regaining his strength and searching his mind for a solution to his dilemma in trying to figure out what his next move should be. He wandered through the village getting to know the inhabitants and thought about doing something to repay the kindness of the McNally's.

He was there less than a week when the town's blacksmith died. It was a tragedy for the village, because he shod all of their horses and had three horses of his own which he lent out to people in the village when they needed a horse.

McNally and a few of the villagers pooled together some pieces of wood with which they planned to fashion a coffin. They planned to get together the next day and build the coffin in McNally's barn. That night Edward cut all the pieces and fashioned a beautiful coffin. On the face of the coffin he carved an anvil. The next morning after the funeral and burial, McNally and some of the townsfolk approached Edward and questioned him about his experiences. They particularly wanted to know if he knew anything about blacksmithing. He told them that he had never actually done any blacksmithing himself but only watched his father work as a blacksmith. This made no difference to any of the villagers. His father was a smith so he was a smith. Edward walked down the street to the blacksmith shop and entered with reverence. He slowly pushed the door open to the shop and began to inventory in his mind the contents. The old blacksmith left a tremendous supply of rods and metal used to make horseshoes. There was a desk with long flat drawers filled with patterns for making all kinds of useful items as well as horseshoes. He found a book with the names of all the horses in town and notes on all their peculiarities including measurements for every hoof. There was enough coal and coke to last an entire year. Scanning the entire shop he discovered a staircase leading to a loft, which led to a very comfortable bedroom with all the amenities needed for his comfort. The old smith had designed the building in such a way that the heat from the forge kept his loft room very toasty in the winter. In the summer a wall would swing closed allowing the heat from the forge to rise and go out of a vent in the roof. Edward felt very comfortable immediately. He did think a few times that the ghosts of the old smith might not like the way his belongings were passed along to Edward. But he never felt anything but comfortable.

Alongside this new shop was a surrey with a wheel broken. Edward looked at the broken wheel and had no clue as to how he could fix it. He searched through all the material and plans that the old smith left behind and found nothing about wagon wheels. McNally came by the next day. He told him that the surrey was his and that he had sent for a wheelwright from another village to come repair the surrey wheel. The next day the wheelwright came and taught Edward how to make a surrey wheel. The wheelwright did not know how to forge a steel ring to go around the wheel, but he knew how to make the wheel.

He told Edward how he made a deal with the old smith to make the steel ring, and he would make the rest. Edward told him that he would be happy to make the same deal, and so he was in business.

He spent his first week firing up the forge and making spoons, forks, butter knives, and a couple of whisks which he took to give to Sarah McNally to repay them for their kindness. When he stayed at their house, he noted that all the utensils were made of wood and quite worn so he felt this was a perfect gift to repay them. When the surrey was repaired, he hooked up one of the horses and drove to the McNally's. McNally was extremely happy to have his surrey back. He told Edward that he planned to go fetch his daughter who teaches school in a town 12 miles away. The village was planning a fall harvest festival, and he was sure that his daughter would like to be there.

The day before the festival Edward was invited to dinner at the McNally's. When he arrived, they were all sitting at the table ready for dinner. There was an empty chair at the table so Edward walked over and sat down. He began to apologize for being late, telling them that he was busy in the shop with McGregor's horse who just threw…at this point he saw across the table McNally's daughter. McNally saw that he noticed her and said, "Allow me to introduce my daughter, Jennifer." Edward was completely stunned. He could not remember what he was saying. Everything else seemed to disappear, all the people in the room, tables and chairs, the room itself. She was looking down at the spoon that Edward had made. When her father said her name, she shyly raised her eyes and looked at Edward and smiled. He looked into the bluest eyes he had ever seen. Her long red hair flowed over her shoulder and down her back. His heart began to pound as if it wanted to jump out of his chest. As hard as he tried, he could not muster one word. She nodded her head and smiled. It was all he could do just to return the smile and nod.

After dinner the McNally family sat around the table asking all sorts of questions about Edward. He began to think back over his life and tell some of the stories about seeing almost the entire known world, his history as a cabin boy, and navigator. They kept him talking late into the night and never seemed to tire as they kept asking more and more questions, wanting to hear more and more stories about the faraway places that he visited as a boy. At one point during the evening Jennifer asked, "Is that a true story?" Edward looked at her and replied, "Yes, absolutely. I would never lie to you; however, let me tell you something you should know about storytelling. Never let the truth stand in the way of a good story."

Later that evening when Edward was leaving, McNally walked over to the door and invited him to church the next morning. Edward accepted graciously and walked back to the blacksmith shop. When he arrived at the shop, he thought back and couldn't remember walking back to the shop or anything he did along the way. All he could remember was Jennifer's face, her blue eyes, red hair that seemed to flow and turn and dive over her shoulder, almost like... like... It was beyond his ability to describe, music? Or waterfall? No, wind. He couldn't think of anything to describe what he felt about her flowing red tresses. He could hardly sleep that night as his mind was filled with the vision he had just seen. Everything he saw reminded him of her.

The next morning he came out of the shop just in time to see the McNally family walking up straight towards the general store/tavern where the people of the village held church on Sundays when the tavern was closed.

After the service as they walked by the blacksmith shop, Sarah McNally asked Edward to have lunch with them and to see Jennifer off to school. The information that Jennifer was leaving created a panicked look on Edward's face, which Sarah picked up on immediately. Sarah giggled and through her smile assured Edward that Jennifer would be back next week for the festival. Red McNally thanked Edward for repairing the surrey, telling him that the surrey was Jennifer's only means of travel and that she would be able to come back for the festival next week now that the surrey has been repaired. He also told him that she was taking one of the horses that he might need in preparation for the festival. After lunch Edward went back to the blacksmith shop and got Jake, one of the horses that the old blacksmith had left behind, and hitched him to the surrey. Jake was the most docile and dependable of all the horses in town. Edward offered his hand and helped Jennifer into the surrey. As her hand slowly slid out of his, he felt as though his heart slid out of his hand and left with her. The family and all the friends and neighbors waved goodbye as Jennifer road out of town up the long slope and over behind the hill. When she went out of sight, Edward looked around and discovered he was the only one standing in the middle of the street.

The next Saturday when Jennifer was scheduled to arrive, Edward walked out of town to the top of the hill and beyond and found a rock to sit on. As he sat, he noticed some mushrooms growing around the bottom of the rock, which he picked and put in his hat. When he saw her coming up the road, he quickly stood up and walked toward the town. When she saw him, she stopped and offered him a ride. He told her he was hunting

mushrooms and gave his hat to her to give to her mother
as they road into town together.

The next two days during the festival they spent
nearly all their time together playing the games that were
set up for the festival, games like bowling over pins, horse
shoes, sack races, ring toss, even a fishing contest in the
pond. They ate corn on the cob, turkey legs, deep-fried
dough and assorted cupcakes and berries. The entire town
was abuzz about the new young couple that everyone
thought was perfect for each other. It was as though the
party was for them as the villagers gave every opportunity
for them to enjoy their time together. When it was time
for her to leave, Edward hooked up Jake and offered to
drive her to the top of the hill so he could finish his
mushroom hunting that she had interrupted two days
before. As they left, nearly the entire village came out to
wave and say goodbye to Jennifer. She left him on the top
of the hill where he would watch her go for over a mile
before she drove out of sight. As she drove out of sight,
the shock of reality came back to him. All he could think
of was that he had to spend another week of waiting
before seeing her again. He went back to his forge and
made cups, knives, forks, spoons, etc.

He soon made a deal with the general store owner to
sell his utensils in the store. He made all these things in
between making horseshoes and taking care of all the
horses' hooves in the town.

The next weekend he found himself at the top of the
hill waiting, thinking of some excuse as the mushrooms
were gone, but she didn't come. He waited until nightfall;
she didn't come. In all of his history and all the things that
he's been through, he never felt as lonely as he did that
night. The next day he inquired when he saw Jennifer's

little sister, Amy, as to why Jennifer didn't come home.
She told him that her school had family day, that she was
in charge and would not be home this weekend.

Edward spent the next week in an internal battle with
himself, knowing that he was wrong, and that he should
not be leading Jennifer down a path that would only lead
to sorrow. He began to convince himself that he was not
infatuated, not in love, not interested in any way in this
lovely blue-eyed, red haired, beautiful creature. He
decided that it cannot be, he must not see her anymore,
before it becomes too serious for him to handle.

When Jennifer came home the next weekend,
Edward made no attempt to see her, staying in his
blacksmith shop, pinging away on the anvil, a sound that
could be heard over half the village as he worked. Jennifer
went back to her school and didn't come back the
following week. Two weeks later she returned, and
Edward stayed in the blacksmith shop looking out the
window every moment to see if he could catch a glimpse of
Jennifer. At one point on that Saturday afternoon Edward
was straining his neck to see out the window of his shop
when the sound of Jennifer's voice came from behind him.
He was leaning on his bucket of water that he used to cool
his horseshoes. When he heard her voice, he jerked and
fell down as the bucket tumbled on top of him soaking him
from head to toe. She laughed as Edward's heart nearly
jumped out of his chest. A laughter that he will never
forget, he was sure, the rest of his life. As he lay there wet
in the straw pile, Jennifer leaned down and wiped his face
with her scarf. The scarf had the scent of one million
roses. The softness of her skin against his face nearly
drove him mad. But he gathered his senses and scooted
backwards up against the wall and said, "You and I, we,
you, we, can't be." "What do you mean?" As tears rolled

up in her eyes, "I couldn't come home. I had things I had
to do, and I had to stay." "No! No, it has nothing to do
with that. It's me, it's me. I can't, I mean we just can't be.
It's impossible." "I thought we were getting along very
well," she said with a puzzled look on her face. "Oh no,
it's not that!" he quickly snapped back. "It's not that at all,
we get along very well. I mean I can't, we can't be
together. You are the most wonderful, loveliest person in
the whole world, and you will have plenty of men who will
be your suitors. You will be loved and have children, and
live a long and wonderful life. It just can't be me as much
as I would… I mean, I would be the happiest man in the
world if you and I could, but we can't, it would be wrong,
we just can't." She sat on her knees in front of him looking
in his eyes and could not believe what she was hearing.
The man who seemed so perfect is now brushing her off
like an annoying bug. He then said as he looked down at
his wet torso, "You should go to school and leave me in my
misery. I wish that I could tell you more. I would like to
tell you everything, but it would break your heart as it has
broken mine. Believe me, it's better this way. Just go and
leave me alone." She stood, slowly turned and walked out
the door. As she turned out of sight, tears flowed down
her face. She cried openly as she ran home.

The next few weeks seemed like 100 years to
Edward. As each day passed, it seemed that another
villager would pass him giving him a dirty look. Soon the
whole village reprimanded him. So much so that he began
to take long walks into the woods and up the mountains
just to be away from the villagers. He found a place high
on a bluff where he thought he could see almost to the sea,
the sea he loved. He entertained the idea of going back to
sea in spite of the dangers that he knew were waiting there
for him. One day when he was sitting on the high bluff, he
began to say her name, "Jennifer, Jennifer, Oh Jennifer."

He started to sing, "Jennifer, Jennifer I want so to love you, I wish I could love you. You have stolen my heart." "Why don't you?" a booming voice echoed out of the woods. It was Red McNally. He walked out of the woods and up on the top of the bluff. He stood in front of Edward saying nothing, just stared in his face with piercing eyes as he took a breath and opened his mouth to speak. Edward spoke first, "I know what you want. I'm sure I can explain in a way that you will understand." "Try me," he said, his chin quivering beneath his beard. "I don't even know where to start." "Start at the beginning, son. I have all day." Edward turned and walked over to a large rock and sat down nodding his head for Red McNally to sit next to him as he began.

He started when he was a small boy, telling how he met his ship owner's daughter and how his captain spoke to her father, who later made it possible to be with his daughter. He told of seeing the navigator hanging in the town square, because he had been seen with pirates, hung by the ship owner the Huguenot. He went on to say that they were married, and on their wedding night, his drunken father-in-law made a bet with other shipbuilders that his ship could get to Venice sooner than theirs could. He told how he sent him off in the night without seeing his bride to guide the ship in the race. He told of his captivity by pirates and how he saved the men by promising Teague that he would stay with him for two years if he would let them go. He told him about finding out that there was a price on his head put there by his father-in-law, the Huguenot. "So you see," Edward went on, "I am married, and as much as I love Jennifer, I cannot break her heart." "So you're telling me that you are married, but you never consummated the union?" "Yes, I never got the chance." Red looked Edward straight in the eye and asked, "Did you love her?" Edward thought for a moment looking at the ground and finally raised his head and said, "I did. It was over six years ago. I was much younger then, and now I can't go back." Red leaned back against the rock, looked up into the sky and said, "That's a dilemma. If I didn't like you so much I would throw you off of this mountain right now, but I know how my daughter feels about you so I feel compelled to help you in some way. That's it! Consummation! Consummation! The marriage was never consummated so you are not married." Edward looked at him saying, "I don't think that would hold up in court." "Court, Court, yes, that's the answer." Red spoke in an excited voice, "I have a friend in Boston who is a lawyer. We must go and visit him. I am sure that he will have an answer."

By this time it was the end of twilight and the beginning of darkness. The sky became slightly overcast, and there was no moon. It was so dark they could not see their hands in front of their faces. They each felt around

and found sticks which they used to swing in front of them
as well as feeling the ground trying to stay on the trail.
They both swung the sticks around, and on two occasions
they hit each other with their sticks so they decided to hold
hands so they would not hit each other. On one occasion
they slipped off the edge of the trail and slid down through
the trees about ten feet. They scrambled their way back up
to the path and continued their journey on hands and
knees in order to get past a treacherous area. They made it
about halfway back when they heard Sarah's voice off in
the distance and saw a swinging lantern. She found them
standing on the trail holding hands, "I see you two made
friends," she said looking at their hands. They both looked
down at their hands, jerked their hands apart, jumping
back from each other so quickly that Sarah laughed
uncontrollably.

The next week Edward and Red saddled up and
headed for Boston. It was a three-day ride. Upon arrival
in Boston the smell of the sea air and the sound of the
ropes straining to hold the ships against the dock was
almost too much to bear for Edward. He could hardly
restrain himself from jumping off his horse and
disappearing in some ship. They found some lodging, then
stopped in at a local pub for dinner. In the morning they
made their way to the office of Brian O'Toole, Attorney-
At-Law. Brian O'Toole was known for winning nearly
every case that he ever had. Edward and Red told their
story in great detail. Of course, Red interjected his idea
that, "The wedding was not consummated. Therefore, it
was not legal or binding." "Consummation," O'Toole
began to explain, "has no precedence in a court of law,
although it's a pretty good argument. Here's what you're
going to have to do. You are going to have to go back to
Alsace Lorraine and get your wife to divorce you."
Edward then told him, "There's a price on my head put

there by my father-in-law." O'Toole leaned way back in his chair and said, "You realize that if it is true that there is a legal price on your head, I am obligated as a servant of the law to turn you in." Edward stated, "I'm not sure it is legal since it was put on me by my father-in-law." "Let me look into it, and I will send you a letter in a few weeks with what I think will be the best solution to your problem." With that the two headed back to their village. About two months later a traveling salesman came to the village carrying a letter for Edward Mullin. As soon as he got the letter, Edward opened it, read it right on the street.

Dear Mr. Mullin:
I have discovered that indeed you are correct in your statement that there is a price on your head. To answer what I am sure is a curiosity, it's for 2,000 pounds. There was another man mentioned in the same notice by the name of Teague. He seems to be a bit more valuable than you are in that they have 5,000 pounds on his head. The bounty is indeed that of an individual and not a legal entity. As for the marriage dilemma, under the laws of England and the American colonies, if a spouse is missing for more than seven years, he or she may be declared legally dead which would free you from your marital vows. Enclosed you will find the legal documents which you must sign on or after the 7th anniversary date of your September wedding. Upon signing this document you must register it at your local government office. Along with this document you will also find my bill.
Yours truly,
Brian O'Toole

    After reading it, he was so excited he jumped up in the wagon with the traveling salesman, kissed him on the cheek, shaking him so much that the wagon began to tip back and forth making things fall off onto the street.

Edward then jumped down off the wagon and ran all the way to McNally's house. When he arrived, he was so excited and winded that he couldn't speak so he shoved the letter into Red's hand. He read the letter while Edward was trying to catch his breath and then said, "I knew it! I knew it! I told you O'Toole was the best, didn't I?" as he gave the letter to Sarah. "Where is Jennifer?" Edward managed to squeeze out through his heavy breathing, "Where is she?" Sarah answered, "She is at school, it's Thursday. She won't be home until Saturday, if she decides to come." "This can't wait," Edward yelled as he grabbed the letter from Sarah's hand. He then turned and ran to the blacksmith shop and saddled the fastest horse. As he galloped threw the town, he noted a few dirty looks from local residents, but he just smiled at them and yelled, "Yahoo," as he swung his hat around and around over his head.

Arriving at Jennifer's schoolhouse, he road the horse around the building from window to window looking in and yelling, "Jennifer, Jennifer!" Jennifer was teaching class and paid no attention to the madman in the windows bobbing around on his horse. Edward rode his horse around back and up the other side to the window nearest Jennifer's desk. His horse continued to bob around as he tried to look in the window yelling, "Jennifer, Jennifer!" The children were giggling at this point. Jennifer tried to calm them and told them to get back to work while she turned and opened the window. She leaned out the window far enough so that the children could not hear the conversation with Edward. Edward put his arm around her and pulled her out of the window onto his horse, which prompted all the children to run to the window and put their heads out.

As the horse finally began to calm down, Edward found that he also had to calm Jennifer. She was somewhat disheveled and distraught over having been dragged out of the schoolroom window. She struggled and pushed her way out of his arms and down to the ground. She straightened her dress, stomped her foot on the ground, and yelled, "Mr. Mullin, you are a very strange man. One day you like me, and the next day you tell me to get lost. Then, you come here and drag me out of the window." Edward started to get down off the horse, but she pushed him back on and continued, "With no good reason and you expect me to enjoy the way you are treating me? Go back to where you came from. I will be home this weekend. You owe me an explanation that will have to wait until then. For now, get lost." She turned and stomped off around the corner of the school and back inside where he could hear her telling the children to get back in their seats.

Edward road back to the village. He stopped at McNally's and talked to Red saying, "I think I am in trouble." Red looked at him with a puzzled look and asked, "Now what? I thought we just solved all your problems." "Well," he then recounted to Red and Sarah what he had just done. They both sat there and looked at him with their mouths open for a moment. Red finally shook his head up and down and said, "Yeah. You're in trouble." Red assured him that when she came home Saturday that he would talk to her and see what he could do. Edward spent the next day trying to get some work done, but he just walked around the shop banging into things and knocking them over. Saturday was even worse. He couldn't get his mind off of the stupid thing that he did. He decided that Jennifer would think that he was working if she heard the hammer hitting the anvil. He sat bouncing his hammer on the anvil almost in a stupor when all of a sudden the door banged open. Jennifer ran in, jumped on him, wrapping her legs around him and her arms around his neck, knocking him backwards onto a pile of straw behind the horses. She then laid on top of him, kissing him all over his face and ending up on his lips. Her long red hair fell down all around his head and caressed it as she kissed him. Her soft voice murmured, "I love you." Edward tried to say, "I lo..." but she kept on kissing him. He laid there totally immersed in the most tender moment he had ever known. She sat up on her knees and tried to pull him up, but he refused to sit up. "Come," she said. "Let's go have lunch." "I can't. You go ahead. I will be there shortly." "No! Come now, my parents are going to take us to lunch." "I can't," he said. "Now what's the matter?" She asked in an almost harsh voice. He laid there for a moment and then replied, "Well, okay, I will

never ever keep anything from you again. I'm lying in
horse manure."

        "What!" She pulled him up. Sure enough his back
was completely covered with horse manure. She sat back
and laughed for a whole minute. She then helped him out
of his shirt, put her finger in the manure, and put some of
it on his nose. He was shocked as he asked, "What was
that for?" "That was for pulling me out of the
schoolhouse window," she answered. "Now we are even."
She then helped him clean up. He put on a clean shirt, and
they started out the door. Just then he grabbed her and
pulled her back into the shop behind the door. He
wrapped his arms around her, and they kissed for over a
minute. Then they walked hand-in-hand down the street
towards McNally's house. As they walked by several
houses, he noticed the people who had frowned at him in

recent days now had broad smiles. When he saw this, he looked at Jennifer and said, "I never want to be without you again." "Me too." She smiled. The McNallys then took Edward to the tavern/grocery store/church/restaurant where they had a fine luncheon.

After lunch they went back to McNally's house and sat at the kitchen table where they made small talk for a few minutes. Edward then said to Red, "I am so happy that you talked to Jennifer." At this statement Red got a sheepish grin on his face. Seeing this, Edward said, "You did talk to her, didn't you?" "Well," Red trying to explain, "I tried. I mean I was going to, but I only got so far as to tell her that you loved her and wanted to spend your life with her then she bolted out the door. I yelled after her that we planned to take you out for lunch." Edward's mouth dropped open, "So you didn't tell her?" "Tell me what?" Jennifer demanded. "It's, it's, well," Edward stammered and finally began, "it's a long story." Jennifer leaned back in her chair and said, "Humor me." "Well I have to start back when I was young." Red interjected, "Really young." Jennifer looked askant at her father then back at Edward. He went on, "On one of my trips to Venice I met a girl. She was young." Red jumped in again, "Young, really young." This time his wife Sarah turned and gave him a dirty look. Edward went on, "She was the daughter of the Huguenot man who built and owned the ships that I was working on. I liked this girl a lot." Again Red jumped in, "He loved her." "Well, at this point I just liked her. I was just a cabin boy, and she was the shipbuilder's daughter so she was in a different class than I was. There was no chance that her family would accept me. So my Captain talked to her father and convinced him that he should meet me. So, well, he liked me, and he wanted to introduce me to his daughter. Later we got engaged." At this point he hesitated. Jennifer leaned forward even more saying, "Yes, go on," with the sound of skepticism in her voice. "Well," hesitating again. Red squirming in his chair blurted out, "He married her." Jennifer's mouth fell open as she looked at her father then back at Edward. Edward lowered his head and nodded yes. As Sarah backhanded Red in the chest, Jennifer's eyes welled up with tears. She stood up, sliding her chair back, stomped her foot on the floor, turned and started for the door. Red yelled after her before she reached the door, "He's a virgin." She stopped dead in her tracks, wiped the tears from her eyes, then turned slowly around and walked back to her seat, slowly sitting down. She put her elbows on the table, and one hand on each cheek with her chin in her palm saying, "This has got to be good, please continue." There was no lack of sarcasm in her voice. "Well," Edward hesitated again and then continued, "We had a big wedding. Afterwards there was a big party at the Huguenot's mansion. The party lasted way into the night. The Huguenot, drunk out of his mind, challenged two other shipbuilders to a race to Venice. He directed his bodyguards to make sure that I was the navigator. They grabbed me from the party and took me to the ship which left immediately." Red jumped in again and said, "Consummated, the marriage was never consummated." Jennifer then said, "So you ran away to America." "No, I had every reason to stay. Her father was going to build a mansion for us and make me the Captain of the biggest ship he had ever built. I had no reason to leave. I was captured by pirates." "Oh," she was more skeptical than ever, "I suppose you were captured by Captain Teague." Edward looked surprised and asked, "How do you know that?" "Teague is the most famous pirate there is," she couldn't believe her ears, "You expect me to believe this story?" "Yes," he insisted, "it's true, I swear it's true!" "You two sat up there on that hill and made up this story," as she stood up, stamped her foot on the floor and turned to leave again. "No, no!" Edward reached into his pocket and pulled out the letter, "here I have proof." She took the letter from his hand and looked at the envelope. "Boston! You went to Boston?" She inquired. Red jumped in again, "We both went." "It's a three-day ride to Boston." "And three days back," Edward added. "And you went to see a lawyer to prove to me that you are married?" Her eyes began to tear up again. "No, no!" Edward insisting, "Read the letter." She slowly opened the letter and unfolded it. Almost immediately her voice screeched out in a high tone, "You have a price on your head? 2000 pounds?" "No, not that part." Edward insisted, "Read the rest." Jennifer then read on, "It was Teague," she said to herself as she read the rest of the letter and looked up at Edward saying, "September." Edward nodded his head, "September." She looked across the table at Edward's eyes trying to discern whether he was lying or not. His face slowly turned into a broad smile as he tilted his head to one side in a half shrug. She could not help herself as she to begin to smile. Edward then reached into his pocket and pulled something out which he held tightly in his hand for a moment. "I made something for you," then he slowly opened his hand exposing his palm. "It's a ring I made in the shop for you. Since I won't be free until September I made you a friendship ring." Her eyebrows pushed down over her eyes as she looked across the table at him, "A friendship ring?" "Yes, I made it for you." She slowly rose to her feet again and patted her foot on the floor, "Mr. Mullin, I am not a little girl like my students. I am a grown woman. I expect that when the time comes you will not give me a steel ring that you hammered out in your shop. Until September, I will allow you to ask me out and spend time with me. When September comes, we will talk." She then took the letter and went to her room saying as she walked, "I am tired, and I want to lie down for a while." She went into her room, closed the door, and fell fast asleep.

Nothing was said for a few minutes, and then Red broke the silence, "Well, that went well." Edward looked at him and asked, "You think so?" Red said, "Kind of." They both looked at Sarah, and she inquired, "Would you like some pie?" It was late October. Nearly all the trees in the area displayed themselves in many hues of red...red, the color of her hair. It was everywhere. Everywhere he looked things reminded him of her. He could bring to his mind every moment that he spent with her--the slightest thing, the leaf blowing across the floor, the manure on a straw pile, and the sound of the surrey wheels on the street. Edward talked to himself, "I can't lose this girl. I must do better. I have to stop doing all those dumb things. I have to learn to think before I do something." He put his hand in his pocket and felt the steel ring that he had made for her. He took it out of his pocket and looked at it for a minute. He remembered that Captain Teague had nailed a man's ear to the mainmast to remind them never to cross him. He then took his hammer and a nail, and nailed the ring high on the post between the stalls as a reminder not to do stupid things.

As the days grew shorter and the snow came, Jennifer came home less frequently, because the roads were too deep with snow for the horse to pull the surrey. Edward walked out of town every Saturday and sat on the rock on top of the hill watching for Jennifer to come around the bend. He was there every Saturday, even the Saturdays when she didn't show up. On those Saturdays he would wait for hours even in the cold and snow.

Edward took a long flat bar of steel, polished it to a high polish, bent it up to fit the front wheels of the surrey and fastened it there. He then ran it flat on the ground under the back wheel and fastened it to that wheel. This turned the surrey into a sleigh. He put beeswax on the runners and pushed it out of the shop. When he did this, it slid all the way across the street.

He then took the sleigh to Jennifer's house. She was very excited and couldn't wait to ride in the sleigh. When she opened the door and saw what he had done, she ran out and jumped into the sleigh without getting her coat or boots. "Take me for a ride," she screeched, "take me for a ride." Edward had put several blankets in the surrey to keep her legs warm. He bundled her up in the blankets, opening his coat, pulled his right arm out of the sleeve, and put her right arm in the coat sleeve, then pulled her in close to his chest. Jennifer's legs were not long enough to reach the floor of the surrey so Edward built a box for her feet. He put blankets and other things he thought she might need in the box. She was so excited that she yelled and waved at everybody in town who was on the street, "Look what Edward made for me. My surrey is a sleigh." Jake, Edward's horse, had slipped and fallen twice trying to pull the surrey through the deep snow. Now it moved

so easily over the snow that Jake seemed to like the sleigh
more than Jennifer did, because he kicked up his heel
several times while pulling them around the village.

The next Sunday morning Edward was walking
downtown to get something to eat. When he arrived at the
tavern, he heard Jennifer's laugh. He looked through the
window to see Jennifer sitting across the table from a man.
He watched them through the window for a while as they
had a very long conversation. He went back to his shop
and paced up and down with all sorts of wild thoughts
going through his brain. He didn't accompany her to the
top of the hill as he usually did. The next Saturday when
she came back he was not sitting on the rock. Jennifer
passed her house and drove straight to the blacksmith
shop. She thought he might be ill and would need her. He
was hammering on his anvil, making a horseshoe, when
she came in. She ran up to him and said, "Are you okay?"
"Yes, why wouldn't I be?" He looked down his nose at
her. She cocked her head a little bit with a questioning
look on her face and said, "You weren't on the rock, so I
thought something was wrong." "No," he said, as he
turned and picked up the horseshoe again with his tongs.
She bent down, ducked under his arm and came up
between him and the anvil. "What is it?" Pushing her
body against his front and looking straight up into his face,
"What is it? Tell me." He looked down at her and his eyes
began to get misty. "I saw you with a man last week."
"What man?" She demanded. "In the tavern last Sunday.
He was laughing and having a great time." He began to
choke up a little. She thought for a second and then said,
"Sunday, Sunday, that was Brian." He wobbled his head
from side to side, "Brian, that was Brian. I'm going to
smash him in the face," his legs spread apart and his fists
on his hips. "Well, Edward Mullin, you are jealous," she
smiled a sheepish grin. "Me! Jealous, I'm not..." She cut

him off, "Yes you are." She jumped up, straddled her legs around his waist, hugging his neck and kissing him all over his face, and again ending up kissing his lips. After a minute or so he put his hand on her waist and set her feet on the floor. Then stood there with his feet apart and his fists on his hips, demanding, "Tell me about Brian." She mimicked his pose with her fists on her hips and feet apart. She looked up into his face and began to explain, "He is a colleague of mine. He teaches school here in our village on Tuesday and Thursday. He teaches in a different town on Monday and Wednesday. Once a month we get together and coordinate our curriculum so that all the students in our county are learning the same thing. He is also our minister, and he preaches at 8 o'clock every Sunday in the tavern. If you would come to church with us, you would already know him. He also has a girlfriend with long blonde hair, long legs, blue eyes and a perfect complexion." "Oh, I didn't know." Looking at her with an apologetic face, "Are you mad at me." "No," she looked at him with a broad smile, "I am flattered really. I'm glad you were jealous." "Oh really," he smirked, once again striking his fists on hips pose. "Yes, it shows how much you love me." He looked at her for a moment and smiled, then snickered a little bit saying, "You said she was blonde with blue eyes?" "Yes." "Tall, perfect complexion, long legs?" he went on. Jennifer spit in her palm, doubled up her fists, rubbed it in the spit saying, "I'm going to smash her in the face!" He wrapped his arms around her, picked her up until her elbows were on his shoulders and when her hair brushed against his cheeks, he fell in love with her all over again.

The next Sunday morning Edward forced himself out of his warm bed, put his feet on the cold floor, and shuffled through a drawer trying to find his best clothes. Heavy snow had fallen the night before. He had to force his door open against a snow bank, which had formed against the outside. He begrudgingly drudged his way up the snow-covered street to attend services in the tavern. Brian's sermon was on the creation. Edward listened attentively. After the services Edward and the McNally's invited Brian to have lunch. After lunch they sat in the tavern, and Edward listened as Jennifer and Brian spoke about their school children. There was a short lull in the conversation, and Edward spoke. "So Brian, you really believe in this God thing, don't you?" Brian with a surprised look replied, "I do." Edward asked, "Why?" Everyone at the table appeared shocked as they looked at Edward and wondered what would come next. Brian looked at him and said, "Look all around you. We have air to breathe which all the plants around us create so we can live. We breathe out carbon dioxide, which the plants use so they can live. Your body, for example, is a complex machine. You eat food that goes into your system, which turns it into your muscles, your bones, your eyes, your hair. The universe and everything we know works together in harmony. None of these things could happen by chance." "Well," Edward thought and then went on, "Maybe it could happen." "Let's see," Brian thought as he looked up at the sky and then down at his watch, "You are mechanically inclined. Let's say, that by chance, by some strange chance that all the parts of this watch existed. No one made them. They just exist. Let's say you found all those parts, and you put them in a bag and shook the bag. How long would it take and how many shakes would it take until you open the bag to find a perfect operating watch?" Edward had his elbow on the table, and he put his chin on his fist while he looked across the table back at Brian. "Hmmm," he hesitated then acknowledged, "Never, probably," as he shifted his head from his fist to his palm. Brian went on, "So you see there has to be a plan, a preset plan. Then it has to be carried out or put together by its creator before it can work." Edward sat there for a while deep in thought. Then Brian asked, "What do you think?" Edward looked up and said, "Well, there must be something to it, because you make a living talking about it." Brian laughed out loud for a minute and then said, "For you, Edward, no charge."

Over the next two months Jennifer missed coming home a few times because of the heavy snowstorms. One cold winter day a stranger rode into town. He stopped at the tavern and asked Joe if he knew where he could find Edward Mullin. Joe poured him a drink and told him he could find him at the blacksmith shop. He then told his son to run down and tell Edward that a stranger was looking for him. On the way down Joe's son saw his girlfriend, and she invited him in for some hot cocoa. After drinking the cocoa he walked down towards the blacksmith shop. About 20 feet from the shop he heard a gunshot. He quickly ran down beside the shop and peered through the window where he saw the stranger wrapping Edward up in a tarpaulin on the floor. Then he saddled Edward's horse. He lifted the body up, put it over the horse, and tied it on. He mounted his horse, tied the reins to his saddle, and slowly walked down the main street up the hill and out of sight. The boy ran back to the tavern and told his father what he had seen. Joe gathered together a few of the men in the bar and a few others from across the street and told them what had happened. They all dispersed, saddled their horses, and met a few minutes later in the street in front of the tavern. As they turned to head out of town, they saw walking over the hill towards town Edward's horse with the tarpaulin sack hanging over it and another horse in tow dragging a man behind it whose foot was caught in the stirrup. It was the stranger leaving a long trail of red drops leaking from a hole in the side of his head. They rode up the hill, untied the tarpaulin, and put it on the ground. When they untied and opened the tarp, they found Edward with a bullet hole in his upper left shoulder. One man yelled out, "He is still alive." They all carried him to McNally's house. They put

him on the kitchen table where Red began to dig out the bullet. Red's wife cauterized the wound with a hot poker. During the next three days Edward was delirious. He woke up several times yelling "no", sweating and shaking from being cold. After the third day he began to heal quite rapidly. By the end of the week Sarah had nursed him back to health.

In the meantime the villagers sent for the magistrate from Riverside to investigate what had happened. After questioning nearly everyone in town he found no answer to the mystery of how the stranger came to his end. He found out that the stranger was a bounty hunter. In view of this fact he decided no more investigation was necessary. The reason for the stranger's demise will remain a mystery. When Edward was able to talk, the magistrate questioned him and told him the stranger's horse and saddle were in the blacksmith shop. Because of what had happened he could see no reason to impound the animal, instead he gave it to Edward.

Three weeks later when Jennifer was finally able to return to the village the incident was all but forgotten. On the occasions when Jennifer was unable to come home, Edward spent most of his time with Brian. They were fast becoming great friends. When Brian came into town to preach and teach, he stayed with different families in their homes. It was getting to be a problem in the congregation figuring out who would be next and where he would stay. On occasion he had to stay in a boarding house, which he could not really afford. Edward fixed up another bunk in his loft above the shop.

The two spent many evenings in conversation, playing cards, and sharing recipes for things they could cook on Edward's steel melting fires. Edward expressed his discomfort about Jennifer's traveling back and forth and missing her on the snowy weekends. Brian began to talk of the possibility of building a church. Edward said it was silly to build a building to be used only one hour a week. He suggested building a schoolhouse and noted that there were two new families who just moved into town that had four children altogether, which meant he would be teaching seven students instead of three. He felt that plus being able to use it for church services was reason enough to call a meeting and get the villagers to chip in to build a public building. The following Sunday Brian suggested from the pulpit that the people of the town get together and build a municipal building which could be used for town meetings, schooling the children, and for church on Sunday. The villagers were very interested.

In the following weeks Edward and Brian drew the plans for the construction of a new schoolhouse that would also serve as a new church and town hall. One day while Brian and Edward were drawing plans, Edward looked up and said, "You know, of course, there is a method to my madness." "Yes," Brian smiled, "I know you're trying to get rid of the schoolteacher, me." "Well, I wasn't going to put it that way. It's just that I worry about Jennifer traveling back and forth. It would be much better if we could have her here." Brian very understandingly replied, "Let's see if we can do something about that." There weren't enough students in the village to warrant a full-time teacher so Edward began to ask questions of everyone who came into town from the countryside about how many children they had. He discovered there were four children who lived within two miles of the village who did not go to school. With the three children they already had, the four that just moved in, and the four from the countryside, they would have enough students to warrant a full-time teacher. The plans were to start construction the minute the snow melted in the spring. Once the construction was complete Brian would ask for a transfer to Jennifer's school. They would then ask the villagers to hire Jennifer full-time.

The winter's grip finally gave way, and miles of white finally turned to shades of green as the birds returned. But it wasn't over yet. The winter's madness and deep melting snow swelled creeks and rivers, and knocked out a bridge causing Jennifer to have to turn around and go back over the squishing muddy road that was a foot deep in places. Jake was once again unhappy slopping, splashing, and slipping his way through the muck. When the word came that the bridge was out, the men of the town got together and went out to rebuild the bridge. Jennifer told her students, who told their parents of the problem, and they went out to rebuild the bridge. Because they were able to work from both sides at the same time, construction went very rapidly. The two villages working together had the added plus of forming new friendships and bonding the two villages together.

The time came when the children were getting out of school for the summer, and Jennifer was coming home to stay. Construction of the building was almost complete. Edward was busy working in the shop making a mold and melting enough steel to make a bell for the small steeple that was constructed on the front of the peak. On the day of the pour, all the kids of the town and several men were there along with Jennifer and Brian. Jennifer held the long rod that held the crucible. Edward was on the other end turning it to pour the molten steel in the mold. While the steel cooled, the ladies of the town set tables outside of the blacksmith's shop full of food and had a great party.

Two hours later Edward broke the mold off of the bell revealing the letters that he had molded in the metal, Jennifer. The next day the whole village came out to watch the raising of the bell. Edward and Brian were up on the roof. They pulled the bell up on a rope. They mounted it inside the small steeple and tied a rope on the swing-arm, then threw it down the front of the building. Everyone decided that Jennifer should be the first to ring the bell. When she pulled the cord for the first time, Edward and Brian were holding it tightly so nothing would happen. She pulled even harder and still nothing. She reached up high on the rope and grasped it as tightly as she could. The two men lifted her up until her feet were about three feet off the ground, much to the delight of everyone watching. She finally rang the bell and got them back by ringing the bell over and over, making them put their fingers in their ears as everyone applauded. One of her little students looked up and said, "Oh no! Edward has just hung Jennifer in the steeple."

One man yelled out, "Let's all go in and have our first town meeting. We're all here." So they all filed in and filled up the room. One of the men said, "Brian, you run the meeting, you have the most experience." So Brian got up on the small stage in front and stood behind a makeshift podium, banged his knuckles on the podium saying, "Call the meeting to order. What will be the first order of business?" There was a moment of silence and finally one of the men said, "Let's hire Jennifer for our teacher." Everyone but one man seemed to agree. He held up his hand and was recognized by Brian, "What about you, Brian? Aren't you going to be out of a job?" "Well, I was hoping to get a letter or two recommending me for Jennifer's old job." The man smiled and said, "No problem." There were small discussions in the room, and Brian again rapped his knuckles, "We have a motion on the floor to hire Jennifer as our schoolteacher. Are there any questions?" One of the men in the hall stood saying, "We only have three students. How can we afford a full time teacher?" Edward then raised his hand and was recognized, "Actually we have 11 students, adding four from the new family who just moved in and four from local farmers who live less than two miles from our village." The man still standing said, "Oh, in that case, we do need a full time teacher." A woman held up her hand and said, "How many students does she have over in Riverside?" Jennifer spoke, "I have 18 students." The lady then asked, "How much are you paid over there in Riverside?" Edward quickly jumped up and shouted, "Seven dollars a month!" Jennifer looked at him astonished that he would say anything about how much she made. "Oh," the lady said, "since we have only 11 students here and you're paid $7.00 for 18 students, I would suggest since we are a poor community that $6.00 might be a better price." Jennifer squirmed in her chair and tried to stand up, but Edward pulled her down and held her hand. Brian then said, "Are you making that a motion?" The lady nodded. He then went on, "I have a motion for $6.00 a month. Do I hear a second?" Someone seconded, and Brian called the vote. It was unanimous. Jennifer again tried to stand, but someone in the room yelled out, "I make a motion that we adjourn." Brian asked, "Is there a second?" There was an immediate second, and the meeting was over.

As everyone began to leave the room, Jennifer jumped to her feet and yelled, "Wait a minute." There was a lot of noise in the room so Edward said very loudly, "Jennifer would like to say thanks." Everyone standing at this point turned around, looked at Jennifer, and said almost in unison, "Thank you, Jennifer." Then Edward began to clap his hands, and the whole crowd applauded then turned to walk out. As they walked out the door, there were many people milling around and talking to each other. As they walked through them, almost everyone near them congratulated Jennifer saying, "Thank you. We are glad you are our teacher." They walked down the street towards her house. When they got out of earshot from the crowd, Jennifer demanded, "How could you do that?" "Do what?" putting on his most innocent face. "You lied to them," she insisted. Edward stopped walking and looked down at her, "I didn't lie. That's the way you negotiate. It was a negotiation. If you want to ge...." "It was a lie," she continued to insist. "Jennifer, it's a tactic, not a lie. It's a tactic." He tried to go on and explain, but Jennifer stomped her foot on the ground. Edward has learned that when she stomps her foot, he better listen to her. "Tell me," she said, "is what you said the truth?" "Well, it wasn't true, it was...," he hesitated, "it was a white lie." "A white lie!" she repeated, "A white lie! What in the world? It doesn't matter what color it is, a lie is a lie." "Jennifer, if I hadn't said that, you would be working for $4.00 a month." Just then, Noreen the town busybody was walking by. Jennifer called her over and said to her, "Noreen, I feel just terrible." Noreen moved in between Edward and Jennifer. Edward was standing behind her making all sorts of gestures, slicing his neck with his hand, putting his finger over his mouth, shaking his finger back and forth, trying to get her not to say anything without letting Noreen see his actions. Jennifer went on anyway, "Edward has told everyone that I was making $7.00 a month, when I was only making $5.00." Noreen looked shocked as her mouth fell open, and she took a quick breath. She then leaned down and whispered in Jennifer's ear, "Jennifer, no one needs to know that. You are worth every penny of $6.00; it should have been $7.00. I promise you that I will work on getting you $7.00 next year." She then stood up straight, nose in the air, and slowly turned to look at Edward. She then took a deep breath and spoke through her nose, "Hmm," turned and walked away. Edward rolled his head around and around and started walking while he talked. "That was Noreen; she has the longest nose in town. She knows everybody's business, and she tells everybody else about everybody and all of their business. She comes over here and puts that long nose of hers in your ear… gossip… stories… innuendos… exaggerations. Why she's going to tell everybody in town. I'll bet half the people know already. Why, she spreads rumors around like peanut butter on crackers. She's going to be talking about us from now until…" Jennifer jumped in front of him and made him stop. "Do you know what she told me?" asked Jennifer. He screwed up his face and answered, "I know what she said, she's one of the nastiest people in the…" Jennifer stopped him again, grabbed his ear and pulled it down to her mouth and told him what Noreen had said. Edward straightened up, raised his eyebrows high on his forehead, tilted his head to one side, and began to walk slowly as he said, "That Noreen is one of the nicest people in this village. She is a sweetheart. She is kind and generous. She takes care of her own. Why, she's a sweetie. If you were new in this town, she'd be the first one you should get to know. She would take care of you. Why, she's one of the kindest… gentlest… greatest… open minded… wonderful…

To Edward, it seemed like a year but summer finally came, and Jennifer was home to stay. One day Brian came with a request from Jennifer's students in Riverside who wanted to have a going away party for Jennifer. When Joe the bartender at the tavern heard of the trip, he asked Edward to pick up a case of assorted whiskies and bring it back for him. Edward hitched up Jake and picked up Jennifer early one Saturday morning and left for Riverside. Jake knew the way so Edward just held the reins in his hand and turned all of his attention to Jennifer. They hugged, kissed, talked, laughed, and Jennifer told stories about all of her kids that he was about to meet.

When they arrived there was a large group of people who led them to the park, where they had a great feast and all sorts of games to play. They celebrated the time they had with Jennifer as their teacher. Each student gave her a gift, all sorts of things that they had made as well as perfume and soaps, etc.

At the end of the party, they headed back with just enough time, they thought, to get back before nightfall. About halfway back, huge black clouds rolled in over the hills and filled the sky above. The wind began to swirl and pick up the dust in the road. Jake began to get fidgety and very nervous. Just then a huge lightning strike hit a tree in front of them. It cracked and crashed across the road blocking their path. Jake reared up, jerked away, snapping the linchpin, and then bolted off into the woods. Then huge drops of water began to hit the top of the surrey as Edward quickly rolled down the isinglass curtains to keep them from getting wet. The rain came down so hard in such large drops they could hardly hear each other even if they yelled.

They bundled up close together and wondered what to do next. Then Jennifer said, "My emergency box!" Edward looked at her and said, "Yes," remembering the box he built into the surrey so that she could put her feet on something solid, preventing her from bouncing off of the seat when the wheel hit a bump. Since it was a box, Edward decided to put things in it that she might use in an emergency. He had an extra blanket for when it was cold, a rain poncho, as well as a large tarp for Jake in case of a large rainstorm. He also had a shovel, a shotgun and shells, a lantern and a small can of fuel, beef jerky, some crackers, a first aid kit, and some rope.

When the rain subsided a little, Edward opened the box and pulled out the tarpaulin, draped it over the seat, and used the rope to tie it down around the bottom making a kind of tent over the whole surrey bed. While he was tying the tarp down, Jennifer opened the box and pulled out the heavy, thick, coarse blanket and laid it on the bed of the surrey. She then pulled her warming blanket out and put it over the top of her. She lay in the bed waiting for him. Edward made a small opening in front and got in with some difficulty, took off his shoes, and slid in under the seat and under the blanket with Jennifer.

They listened to the wind howl and the rain pummel the surrey roof. Then suddenly a very strong wind ripped the roof off the surrey. The rain then splattered the tarpaulin. Jennifer said, "I'm hungry." Edward said, "Haven't you ever looked in this box?" "Not really," she answered, "You told me there were blankets in there, and I believed you." "Well," he smiled and reached up and opened the box. He rummaged around and brought out the beef jerky, the marmalade and the crackers, as well as the matches, a small lantern, and a can of fuel. He hung the lantern on the back of the seat, lit it, and opened the marmalade. She smiled a broad smile. They had a little picnic in the back under the tarp.

After a while Jennifer said, "I'm thirsty." Edward had noticed that there was a puddle forming on top of the tarp causing a little bulge down by their feet. He thought when he saw it that he would kick it to get the water off, but when she said she was thirsty, he pushed a small opening in the side under the tarp and told her, "Empty one of those bottles from Joe the bartender's box and hand it to me when I get outside." He squirmed his way under the seat, put his shoes on, and with some difficulty squeezed out a small opening in the front. He then walked around the side, and pushed his hand up under the tarp. Then he told Jennifer, "Give me the bottle." She didn't answer for a few seconds, and then she said, "It's not empty yet. This stuff is really hot. It's burning my throat." "WHAT!" He tried to peek in the small hole where his hand was, but he couldn't see so he thrust his hand back in the hole and hollered, "Give me the bottle, Jennifer." She put the bottle in his hand, and he squeezed it out of the hole. When he held it up to see how much was gone, he saw only about an inch left on the bottom. He poured the rest on the ground and went around back, dipped it in the puddle, filling it, poured it out, and then filled it again. He pulled the tarp tight again and tied it down, then went back to the front, squirmed his way back under the tarp as rain again began to pummel their tent. He took off his shoes and squeezed under the seat once more and under the blanket. He looked at Jennifer as she smiled a strange smile he hadn't seen before. She lifted her upper lip as she wrinkled her nose and squinted her eyes. She held up another bottle, "This one is better than that one." She had opened another bottle, and over a quarter of it was gone. She began to blink her eyes heavily and began to speak with a slur, "My thung is thick." Edward wasn't sure what to do as he took the bottle away from her and put it back in the box. "We're going to have to pay for that." "Done weary I can af..ard it." Edward began to laugh as she rambled on. "You got me that sat... cat... fat raise so I can drink whatever I wann." She wobbled her head from side to side and blinked her eyes trying to clear her vision. She looked at Edward, "Yoooou are a hand thumb man, a hand thumb man. Did anyone ever swell you that?" Edward held up his hand and looked at his thumb saying, "Hand thumb?" "Noooo, not hands thumb, hand thumb," she hiccupped, "hand thumb." He smiled and said, "I think you are beautiful." "Ha, Ha, Ha how wooold you know, you are a vurrginn." She hiccupped again. She then rolled over and put her face close to his, nearly knocking him out with her breath, and said, "I wav voo... I wav voo." Her head crashed on his chest, and she fell fast asleep. Edward drank some of the water that he had gotten and laid there listening to the rain as it changed from a storm to a gentle spatter. He reached up and turned the lantern off.

The next thing Edward knew the tarpaulin was being torn off. Red McNally was standing at the end looking inside. Jennifer sat up and said, "Daddy," as she reached out and grabbed her father's hand. When he pulled her up on her knees, she threw up over the back of the surrey.

Her father jumped out of the way just in time. Sarah was worried so she sent Red out early in the morning to see what he could find out. He went to the blacksmith shop and found Jake still in harness with a broken linchpin. He looked around the shop and found another pin. He then settled his horse, put a rope on Jake, and headed out along the road to look for the couple. Edward and Red hooked Jake back up to the surrey. As the two men helped Jennifer onto the surrey seat, Jennifer's father told him, "You have some explaining to do." He looked at him and said, "I can explain, but you may not believe it." Jennifer looked down at them with squinty eyes holding her hand on her forehead, "Speak in a whisper. Do you have to yell?" Edward climbed aboard, guided the horse around the tree, and back upon the road again. Edward held Jennifer's head as Jake took them home.

The summer burned on. It was one of the hottest summers in years. July melted into August, and August fried everything in its path. The villagers spent many days just lying on the banks of the river cooling off by jumping in every so often.

By the middle of August Edward was getting excited about getting a ring for Jennifer. He saved money all these months so that he could get a ring that would be deserving of Jennifer. By asking around he found out that only Boston could provide such a ring. He, therefore, decided a trip to Boston was in order. About the middle of August he set out for Boston with all the money that he had saved. Three days later he arrived late in the evening, stabled his horse, and inquired about a bed for the night. He was directed to a place about three blocks from the livery. He walked down a pitch-black street towards a boarding house guided by a light in its window. About halfway there he blacked out completely, and his face hit the street.

He woke up in a bed above a tavern down by the wharf. He got up and ran to the window to see a whole long line of ships bobbing and tugging at their moor lines. He had a splitting headache so he went back to bed. As he laid there he thought about his money and began looking for his pants. When he found them, his wallet was in the wrong pocket. Incredibly the money was still there. It was just before dawn when he sat up on the bed and tried to get up. But he was so woozy; he decided to lay back down. Seconds later the door opened, and four men came in. He was too drowsy and couldn't see clearly, but he recognized their voices. When his eyes cleared up, he realized that he knew the four men. They were part of Captain Teague's crew. "Edward," they yelled, almost in unison, "Welcome home, we missed you. How did you get away from the Indians? We're afraid we lost your money when the last ship sank. Once we get under sail you will be rich again in a week. Oh by the way, we're sorry about the lump on your head. We didn't recognize you in the dark. We checked out your funds in your wallet. We saw it was a bit sparse. So Teague added a couple hundred pounds to it. We hope you don't mind." Edward sat there on the edge of the bed with his mind going through many changes of emotions. Edward asked, "Why are you robbing people on the street? I don't remember you doing that before." They answered, "We're just collecting enough money to stock the ship so we can leave." Edward inquired, "I thought you said your ship sunk?" "It did, that's no problem. There are 20 of them outside the door." One of the guys spoke, "You don't look very good. Let's leave him alone for a while so he can sleep it off," he said to his friends. So they left.

Edward immediately got dressed, slowly opened the door and peeked out. There was a walkway, a railing and an open staircase going down into the tavern area. He looked over the rail and saw Captain Teague and five of his men sitting around a table having breakfast. He quickly ducked back into the room, went over to the window, and made his escape by jumping onto the roof of the one-story building next door, crossing it, then climbing down the opposite side. He wanted to get as far away from the wharf as fast as he could when he remembered the ring. So he began to ask people on the street for the nearest jewelry store. He found one, but it was too early. He walked farther down the street, and there were several more jewelry stores. One of the stores had a man bent over with the key starting to open the door. He walked in right behind the man when he opened the door. The man acted very concerned at first until Edward put him at ease by telling him he wanted to buy a diamond ring. This changed his facial expression tremendously. The man showed him several rings, but they all were too expensive until he remembered what the men had said back in the room. So he rifled through his pants pockets and sure enough found over five 100-pound notes and a 50-pound note that they had put in his pocket. Edward then said, "Show me the most expensive ring you have." The man went in the back for a second and came back with a 2-1/2 carat diamond ring. Edward looked at the ring and thought to himself, *"No one would believe me no matter what I told them. But I sure wish I could buy it."* It was huge. It was too huge really. He told the man to give him a 1-carat diamond ring. The man pulled out a perfectly beautiful one-carat diamond. Then the man showed him two matching gold rings to go with a diamond ring. The set cost 25 pounds, more than Edward brought from home, but he had just come into a fortune that he rationalized was his, owed to him by the men who stole five years of his life. Edward then went out in the street. He had no idea where his horse was, so he began to search the streets for familiar sites. He was thrilled, happy, frightened, and scared to death all at the same time as he frantically searched for the livery where he left his horse. He searched for nearly half the day when finally he recognized a street and found the livery. He could actually feel the adrenaline running through his veins; he was so distraught and excited. He saddled his horse, hid the diamond in his boot, and headed back to the village. He still had over 500 pounds in his wallet, and he began to wonder how he was going to explain all that money. He thought he might give it to people along the way or just throw it on the road. He thought of different ways that he might be able to explain it. It was more money than he could make in five years, or even six years. As he rode, many ideas came to him, but none seem to come with an explanation. As a matter of fact, he wasn't even sure that he could explain the size of the diamond. All he knew is that he loved her and that this diamond was worthy of her. But he still didn't have an explanation. He thought of Jennifer stamping her foot on the street looking up into his face telling him to tell the truth. But as he thought about it he felt, "*No one would ever believe the truth*." Particularly since I am famous for telling stories under my motto of never let the truth stand in the way of a good story.

It was a three-day ride, and he never came up with an idea. As he road into town, the word *truth* kept ringing in his head. Since it wasn't September yet and he couldn't get the paper signed yet, he went straight to the shop, hid the diamond, the rings, and the money. He changed clothes and went straight to Jennifer's house. He hadn't seen her for six days, and it seemed like six years. When she saw him, the first thing she said was, "What happened to your head?" He had completely forgotten about his head. Immediately he thought about what to say. He stopped himself when the thought came to mind to tell her that he was mugged, and the muggers put money in his pocket.

He kept thinking the truth, the truth, the truth. I should tell her the truth. I want to tell her the truth. I can't tell the truth. Finally he said, "I really have a bad headache, and I want to lie down, but I had to see you before I did." He kissed her and went back to his shop.

Later that evening Jennifer came to the shop with some food for his dinner. She also had some bandages for the cut on his head and some cool compresses for the lump. She kept asking him what happened. Finally he said, "I was riding along not paying attention when my horse went under a tree and hit my head on a limb, knocking me on the ground. I was embarrassed to tell you that, because I should have been paying attention." After she had left, he laid his in bed wondering, "What color was that lie?"

September 1st finally came. Edward borrowed the log wagon from O'Grady, who owned a sawmill. He wanted to surprise Jennifer with a piece of slate that she could use as a blackboard in the schoolhouse. He drove the team into Riverside and deposited the papers with the local Justice of the Peace. He then rode over to the slate mines and picked up a 500 pound 4' x 10' piece of slate and put it on the log wagon. He drove very slowly and very carefully down the mountain and back into town arriving around 4 o'clock. He rounded up several men in the town, and by 6 o'clock they had mounted the slate on the wall. The next morning Edward and the others were framing the slate with wood when Noreen poked her nose in the door to see what was happening. Edward saw her come, and he walked back to her and whispered in her ear. He knew that one of her favorite things was to have people whisper in her ear. She looked up at him questioning, "How about four o'clock, noon wouldn't give me enough time." Edward hesitated and said, "Four o'clock, I can't wait till four o'clock." "Sure you can," Noreen insisted, "You've waited a whole year. What's another four hours?" "Okay, remember, on the last stroke of the clock, four o'clock." Edward then drew pictures around the edge, and in his best handwriting he wrote a message on the blackboard. He draped a sheet over the board so that he could unveil it later. He then went to Jennifer's house and told her how he had taken care of the paperwork and that he had a surprise for her in the schoolhouse. He had some difficulty getting the timing just right. His shoes kept coming untied, and he had to stop and tie them at least twice on the way up the street to the schoolhouse. At exactly 3:55 pm they walked up the five steps to the front stoop in front of the school and walked in. He bumped into a few chairs and had to straighten them up in an attempt to get the timing just right. Jennifer saw the sheet hanging in front and wanted to pull it off, but he kept her from doing so as he watched the clock ticking in the back of the room. As the clock chimed, followed by four dings, he got down on one knee, held her hands, and asked exactly on the fourth ding in perfect unison with over 60 of the townsfolk outside the windows, "WILL YOU MARRY ME?" At the same moment with his other hand he pulled the sheet off of the blackboard which read '*Will you marry me?*' surrounded by drawings of roses, daisies, little cherubs shooting arrows, hearts and a dozen question marks. The crowds outside froze in their positions and were perfectly silent as they listened for the answer. Broad smiles on the people outside slowly turned to concern as they leaned forward trying to hear the answer. They waited as some of their concerns turned to fear that they had not done a good thing. Inside, Jennifer's eyes filled with tears that ran down over her broad smile. She was so choked up by the sound, the blackboard, and the question that she could not speak. She finally gathered herself together, took a deep breath and screamed at the top of her lungs. "YES, YES!" The crowd outside went wild yelling out, "Yes, Yes, Yes." Everyone was yelling yes, and they all crowded around the front entrance. The couple stepped out of the front door, onto the stoop, to applause and started down the five steps to the street when four men lifted them up on their shoulders and carried them down the street. One of the older boys who was going to be one of Jennifer's new students began to chant, "Yes, yes, she gave her answer yes." "Yes, yes, she gave her answer yes." "Yes, yes, she gave her answer yes." After the second time, half the people were chanting with him. By the third time they were all chanting. By the time they reached the tavern, where Noreen had planned a huge engagement party unbeknownst to Edward, the group had added harmony to the chant. The entire community crowded into the tavern and was served a sumptuous meal. Afterwards the tavern owner came out with a huge cake that said congratulations across the top. Jennifer made sure that everyone had a chance to see her beautiful ring. It sparkled and shone in many colors, and fairly danced on her finger as Edwards thought, "That diamond seems to love her as much as she loves it."

Edward would have married her immediately, but Jennifer felt that she should have a long engagement. "A long engagement? What makes a difference how long it is? I love you. You love me. Let's get married." "Edward," she said softly, "we have to plan the wedding. There's the dress that we have to make, there's the plans, there's a reception, and the place to have a reception, there's lots of things that have to be done. You don't just say I do and jump in the bed." "The last part," he smiled a broad smile, "let's do the last part." "Edward, you know what I mean. We want to have a day to remember, a special time just for us with all our friends and neighbors. Don't you want to have that?" "Yes, of course," he relented. "How soon is it going to be before we get to that last part?" "We'll get to the last part, don't worry."

There was much excitement in the McNally house while Jennifer, her mother, and her sister laid out all kinds of plans for the upcoming wedding. The date changed from early summer to Easter time to Christmas time and back again. They finally settled on Easter when all the flowers would be in bloom. Edward then had the idea to plant over 500 bulbs around the schoolhouse as a surprise in the spring. He went out late in the night and planted the bulbs around the school. Edward waited patiently for the day, hammering away the time on the anvil. Edward decided to look around for a piece of ground to build a house on for his new bride. O'Grady had just logged an area of about 40 acres just behind the school, a large flat field which ran from the river over to the mountain and then up the mountain about 40 feet to a plateau of about three acres. Altogether it was about 40 acres. He felt that the plateau would be the perfect place to build his house. It overlooked the river and the entire town. It included the open field that Edward was found in when he first came into town. The next time O'Grady came into his shop he asked him about the property. O'Grady said, "That's a beautiful piece. I thought about building a house there myself. I don't think you can afford it." Edward inquired, "How much is it?" "Well," he thought for moment, "I suppose I could let you have it for 70 pounds." Edward acted shocked, but inside he was actually excited and thought that was pretty cheap, but he bargained anyway. "How about 50 pounds?" O'Grady smiled and came back with, "60." Edward looked at him, "Will you meet me halfway at 55?" O'Grady held out his hand; it was a deal.

He took Jennifer to see the property. She walked around and picked up some soil and felt it. "What would

you think if I told you it was for sale?" "I would say," as
she laughed out loud, "we could never afford this."
"Well," he said, "what if we made a deal. I've been getting
a lot of business lately. If I make more things to sell in the
store and that put together with my savings, I think we
could do it." "Your savings," she laughed, "what savings?
You spent all your savings on this ring." "Well," trying not
to give himself away, "not all of my savings." "Yeah," she
snickered, "what do you have left, a nickel?" "Let me talk
to him, and we'll see what happens." Jennifer looked out
at the scene and sat on a stump saying, "This would be
truly a dream."

He waited until the next day when he ran excitedly
down the street to Jennifer's house, rapping on the door
and announcing his deal. Jennifer was very worried that
they would not be able to make the payments. She
whispered in Edward's ear, "If we get in trouble, we always
have this ring." "No, Jennifer, no. That ring is yours, and
it will always be yours, no matter what." While Jennifer
was busy planning her wedding, Edward surveyed their
new property and planned the location of their new home.
The survey discovered a large grove of trees up the
mountain behind the plateau that was part of the property.
O'Grady had not logged that area because of the difficulty
getting the logs down the mountain over the steep rocky
slope without damaging the wood. Edward counted the
trees, measured their sizes, and figured out how large a
house he could build using these trees. He then went back
to his shop and began designing log houses. He drew
several designs, and then he showed them to Jennifer. She
liked parts of the design but didn't like any one in
particular. So Edward went back to the drawing board and
took all the parts that she liked and put them into a new
drawing. When he showed it to her, she looked at it for a
long while. He had designed it to be built in stages. He

planned to build on later if it was needed. Edward watched her and began to think she did not like it. After a while she looked up at him with a look of amazement in her eyes. She was almost unable to speak as she choked out, "How soon can I move in?" Edward started collecting fieldstones around his property. When the weekends came, he dug and laid the foundation. It was to be a two-story log cabin with a porch all the way across the front and another porch on the second floor, which overlooked the river to the front and the town to the left. It would utilize all of its assets including a stream that ran out of the mountains and down one side of the property to the river. He drew the plans for damming the little creek high above the house and running a wooden trough down to the house just outside the kitchen window then back out into the stream so Jennifer would have running water eight to ten months a year. Edward worked on the house every minute of his time that he wasn't in his shop. He made a heavy sluice over the rockiest steep parts of the mountain so he could slide the logs down to the plateau. Later he used that sluice to run the water to the house. He cut and piled all the logs at the top of the wooden sluice. When winter came, he ran water down the sluice that turned to ice. This enabled him to slide the logs down the 700 feet to the plateau below. By the time spring came he piled enough logs to construct the major portion of the house. The rest of the cold winter he collected all the things necessary to build his house so that they could start construction right after the wedding. He spent the rest of the winter notching the logs and getting everything ready so that construction would go very quickly. The snow came and buried everything for most of the winter. It seemed that winter would never end. The last big storm came less than a week before Easter. It seemed like spring came in a second, the snow melted away, the grass turned green, and over 500 flowers popped up out of the ground around the school, surprising everyone in the town. Noreen suspected Edward, but he wouldn't tell.

Two days before the wedding Jennifer came running into the blacksmith shop. Edward looked at her and thought that there was a catastrophic problem. She asked him excitedly, "What should I do? None of us can decide what to do. Should I wear my hair up or down?" He looked at her, tilted his head to one side raising one eyebrow and answered, "Why don't you do both?" She straightened up and lifted her eyebrows in surprise, "That would look stupid." "No, no," he retracted his statement, "not at the same time. You wear your hair up at the wedding, and down at the reception." She blinked her sparkling eyes several times, ran up to him and kissed him, then turned and ran off saying, "I knew you would have the answer." Edward shook his head and went back to his hammering on a horseshoe.

The day finally came, and Jennifer walked down the aisle by her father in what was the most beautiful dress Edward had ever seen. Jennifer had chosen her sister to be her maid of honor, and Edward had chosen her brother to be his best man. Edward had wanted Brian to be his best man, but then there would be no one to do the officiating. Brian conducted the ceremony, and everything went off without a hitch.

Afterwards the entire town gathered in the tavern for the reception. The musicians in town performed, two fiddle players, a harmonica player, a guy with a washboard, and another guy playing a washtub bass. The group played while the newlyweds danced. There was a delicious dinner. Afterwards all of her students wanted to see her presents. They decided to open them in front of everyone so they could all see. They received wonderful gifts. Most of which were for the household: pots, pans, dishes, silverware, bowls, etc. Joe, the bartender, gave a bag that contained two whiskey bottles. One was empty and the other one a quarter full with a note that read, *"These bottles were too valuable to sell. I'm sure you know their history well."* There were several envelopes with money, and cards from all of her children and most every family in the village. One of them had no writing on it. She showed it to Edward, and he said, "Open it." When she did, she found two 100-pound notes and nothing else. "Who would give us this?" Edward looked surprised and replied, "That's a good question." She then stood up, held up the envelope and was about to say something, but Edward pulled her back down to her seat saying, "Jennifer, whoever gave this to us didn't sign their name so they probably don't want anyone to know. It's probably a good idea not to let anyone know, because people will be trying to figure out who it is and bug us forever trying to find out. It's unlikely that they would ever believe us when we tell them that someone gave this much money to us." Jennifer thought a minute then folded the envelope and slipped it into Edward's inside jacket pocket. She opened another envelope with two pounds in it from Noreen, which had a note that simply said, *"I got you seven."* The next one she opened was from Brian's girlfriend who Edward had met for the first time at the reception. It contained two one-pound notes and the phrase, *"Please don't smash my face in."*

They danced late into the night. At the end of the party the couple walked together out the door where three teenagers who were students of Jennifer's met them. They were waiting outside with two wheelbarrows. When they came out, they all yelled, "We are going to bell you." Jennifer, with a surprised look on her face, said, "NO." "Oh, yes," they yelled and pushed each of them into a wheelbarrow which they wheeled down the street, back up the street, and back down the street. They let them off at the blacksmith shop. Then they started ringing bells, laughing, clapping boards together, and yelling at the top of their voices, "Congratulations! We're going to bell you all night." They went inside, and Edward closed the door and locked it. He then ran up in the loft, grabbed the sheets and blankets off of the bed, and called Jennifer to come up. He gave her a pair of his pants and a shirt. He instructed her to take off her wedding dress and put on the pants and shirt. She quickly did as she was told. They slipped out the back door grabbing the small lantern and Jake's tarpaulin on the way out. They sneaked down along the river and then across the field up the rise to the plateau where Edward had laid the foundation of fieldstone and built the chimney and fireplace. He spread blankets on the ground inside the foundation. Edward fashioned a tent with a tarp as they listened to the far-off tinkling of the bells around the blacksmith shop.

He then fumbled with a small lantern for a while and finally got it going. As he set it on a rock, he turned and saw Jennifer as he had never seen her before. It was a moment that burned itself in his memory for the rest of his days. They wrapped themselves together in the blankets, like a cocoon, and bound their lives together forever. They awoke once in the night just before sunrise, and could hear in the distance tinkling bells. When the sun came up, they walked down the hill past the schoolhouse where Edward bent down and picked a bouquet of flowers and gave them to Jennifer. One of the boys saw them coming down the street and smacked the other two boys awake. They all sat up and watched the couple come toward them. Their mouths fell open as Edward and Jennifer stepped past them, unlocked the door, and went in. Edward picked up his travel bag, Jennifer's dress, and hitched Jake to the surrey. They went to McNally's where Jennifer picked up her bag, and they went on their honeymoon.

They rode north for several days to the most popular honeymoon spot in North America at that time, Niagara Falls. While they were gone, O'Grady, who Edward had asked to check all of his designs to make sure that everything was right, got a group of men in the town and began constructing phase one of the house that Edward had designed. The couple had a wonderful honeymoon and came home to a wonderful wedding gift. The house was almost complete. The men were working on the roof and were finishing the windows when they got back.

Within a few days they moved in and started looking for furnishings, making tables, chairs, a special rocking chair which Jennifer loved. During this time Edward was pulling out one of the old smith's large flat drawers when it got stuck. He pulled the drawer out and discovered a large sheet of paper crammed in the back behind the drawer. When he pulled it out, it was a drawing of a

chandelier that the old man was planning to make.
Edward thought, *'This was the reason for all of those rods.'*
The old man had laid in a supply of over 500 rods about
10 feet long. Edward had been making knives, forks, and
spoons out of them. He followed the design and made a
beautiful chandelier that he hung in their new home. It
was admired by so many people in town that over the next
two years he made over 50 of them, which he sold to local
residents and put them on consignment in the local grocery
store. When the traveling salesman came, he asked
Edward to make 10 more for him, which he took to other
towns to sell. He then came back with many orders for
more chandeliers. There were so many that Edward had to
order more of the rods.

During this time, Jennifer gave birth to her first baby
boy, Jimmy, named after her father. It was the most joyful
time of her life. Almost one year later she gave birth to
Sarah, named for her mother. About the time Sarah turned
four and Jimmy turned five, Edward's business was
growing by leaps and bounds, and Jennifer was pregnant
with her third child, who was to come at the end of spring.
In midwinter in the middle of Jennifer's pregnancy, her
mother Sarah died. The decision was made to bury her on
their property next to the mountain on one side of the
plateau. The burial site was about 35 feet away from the
path that led down to the town. It was a traumatic
experience and unexpected, but the family handled it well.

In the ensuing months all was well until four weeks
before school was out. Several of her students came down
with the flu that in a few cases turned into consumption.
By the end of that week, because so many of the students
were ill, Jennifer decided to call school off for a few weeks
in an attempt to keep the epidemic from spreading. Jimmy
also came down with the flu. Jennifer immediately took

Sarah to her father's house. She asked him and her sister
and brother to care for her until the epidemic passed.
They used every remedy at their disposal. Nothing seemed
to help. Edward rode to Riverside where there were two
doctors. One of the doctors was an intern who was just
finishing his studies and would soon become a doctor.
Edward asked the intern to come to their village to see
what they could do to thwart the epidemic. He came and
set up shop in the schoolhouse. He treated everyone as
best he could, but there was nothing he could do for
Jimmy. One of his schoolmates passed away on the same
day. Jennifer was weak from staying up every night with
Jimmy. She went into a deep state of depression. Edward
did everything he could to soothe her, but it was
impossible for her to understand why such a thing could
possibly happen. She was nine months into her pregnancy
with only a few weeks to go. She was so weak and
depressed that Edward began to fear for her life. After the
epidemic, the intern had gone back to Riverside.

Edward brought in the local midwife, who had
delivered several babies in the village, to care for Jennifer.
When her time came, the baby was stillborn. Jennifer was
very, very weak and could not contain her sorrow. She fell
into a kind of coma and slept for three days. Edward was
totally distraught and feared he was going to lose Jennifer
also. He did everything in his power to wake her up and
to feed her. When she awoke on the third day, he
managed to get some soup into her between her periods of
sobbing. She blamed herself. No matter what Edward
said, she felt it was her fault. She sobbed, and when there
were no more tears to fall, she simply sat in the rocker and
stared out the window. Minutes turned into hours, and
hours turned into days, and she sat. Every time Edward
got her to speak she spoke of blaming herself. Edward was
at his wits end, and he too was dealing with his sorrow.

He thought that if he brought Sarah back home that Jennifer would be able to get her mind off of what had happened. When he brought her in, Jennifer smiled for the first time in months. Sarah climbed on her lap. Jennifer held her so tightly, squeezing her little body so hard that she began to scream and cry. Edward grabbed her and pulled her out of Jennifer's arm, pushing Jennifer back in the rocker. Jennifer screamed out, "Don't take my baby away, she's my only baby, don't take her away. I want her. I need to hold her." Edward then stopped, walked back to her, and put her in her arms once more. She kissed her many times and held her and began to apologize to her for losing her brother. Edward told her she did not have to say that to Sarah; after all she was only four and didn't know exactly what was happening.

Jennifer then got up and made lunch for the first time in five days. Sarah was playing with her toys on the floor. Edward, with plenty of work to do, went back to the shop. He wasn't there more than an hour when Sarah came running with blood dripping off of her hand, crying and screaming. Her finger looked as though it been hit with a hammer, and her nail was half torn off. He treated her wounds and took her to grandpa's house. He then went back up to check on Jennifer. Once again she sat in the rocker staring out the window. Edward told her about the child running into his shop. She seemed to have no idea of what happened. She didn't know she had gone. Edward then looked down on the floor next to the rocker on the rocking chair and saw a puddle of blood. The shocked look on his face caused Jennifer to look down. When she saw the blood, she jumped up, screamed, and began pulling her hair as tears ran down her face. She was sobbing uncontrollably. Edward didn't know what to do. He tried to hold her, but it only made her worse. He finally managed to get her over to the bed and put her in. She was shaking all over. He stayed with her until she fell asleep, and then went back to the shop.

It was Friday. Brian was there as he was every Friday, early enough to work on his sermon for the following Sunday. Edward told him of all the happenings of last week. Brian said he would go talk to her. About an hour later he came back and said that she seemed perfectly normal though very tired. She had served tea, and the subject of what had just happened did not come up. He felt that this might not have been the time for such a discussion. Then he said, "You know this would be a good time for you to get to know God." "You are a consummate salesman," Edward said with a smile, the first one that he had in a long time.

Brian left for dinner at one of the church members houses. The members took turns feeding him every Friday and Saturday. Edward was almost out of his mind with worry. He decided for the first time in his life to pray. He got on his knees, folded his hands on top of his anvil, and prayed for help for Jennifer. As soon as he stood up, Noreen came into the shop behind him and inquired about Jennifer. Edward completely lost his composure, put his arms around her, his head on her shoulder, and sobbed over a minute. Once he regained control, he told her all that happened in the last few days. Noreen told him that she too had lost a baby, and that there were seven other women in the village who had also lost babies. Edward asked her if she could talk to Jennifer and let her know that she's not alone. Noreen told him that she would come in the morning.

The following morning there was a knock on the door. It was Noreen and seven other women from the village. He invited them in. They all stood looking at him saying nothing. He picked up on the hint, excused himself, and went down to the shop. Over three hours went by, and Edward's curiosity was overwhelming. He walked quietly up to the house and peeked in the window to see seven women screaming, yelling, crying, tears everywhere. One woman was slamming her fists into the bed. All of them seem to be totally hysterical. Edward quickly turned away from the window, slammed his back against the log wall and slid down until he sat on the floor.

He buried his face in his hands, saying to himself, "What have I done? What have I done?"

He quietly slipped off the porch and ran all the way back to the shop. He picked up his hammer, shook it in the air, looked up, and yelled, "I will never speak to you again. You are useless." He then swung the hammer so hard at the anvil that it broke the handle, and the head bounced off onto the floor. He thought, *'As if we don't have enough troubles, now I have a whole town on my back.'* He could not think of what to do. Then he realized he must apologize to the men of the town for what he had

done. So he went out and rounded up all the husbands of
the seven women and asked them to meet him in front of
the blacksmith shop. Within a few minutes the men all
stood in front of the shop. Edward then wanted to explain
what he had seen in his house, but before he could speak,
he noticed the women coming down the hill and walking
up the street. They were talking, laughing, and several
holding hands as they walked. When they got about a
block from their husbands, they saw them standing in the
street. Almost simultaneously they began to run towards
their husbands, wrapped their arms around them, and
kissed them. Jennifer walked up to Edward, looked up at
him, and said, "I'm sorry." Edward said, "You have done
nothing to be sorry about. Nothing you could have done
would have changed anything." Jennifer jumped up,

wrapped her legs around his waist, put her arms around his
neck, and kissed him all over the face. As he put her back
down on the ground, she said, "Make love to me."
Edward then looked to his right at the couple next to them
who had heard what she said. He was a little embarrassed

until the woman said to her husband, "Make love to me."
That couple held hands and ran down the street.

Edward and Jennifer ran into the shop, up the stairs
to the loft, jumped onto the bed and began to pull each
other's clothing off. They were both half undressed when
they heard someone behind them clearing his throat. They
looked around. It was Brian in the other bed who said, "I
have something I must do. If you'll excuse me." They
quickly grabbed the blankets, pulled them over themselves
and peeked out over their fingers as they held a blanket to
see Brian moving down the stairs. As he caressed her, he
felt her body relax beneath him as though all of the pain of
the past was melting away, leaving just the two of them
with a fresh new beginning.

Later, as he held her close to him, he could not
contain his curiosity so he asked, "What happened up
there?" Jennifer hesitated. Edward started to say, "You
don't have to tell me." But she spoke first, "Did you know
that all those women have lost babies?" Edward was slow
to answer, "Really? I did not know that." "Yes," she sat up
on her elbow and looked down at his face while her long
beautiful hair brushed across his shoulder. "We all decided
that we all have large holes in our hearts. We have
absolutely no control over the past. To carry the past in
our hearts, in our brains, or on our shoulders is simply
foolish. We do not have the ability to do anything about
it. We do, however, have a substantial amount of control
over the present. We also have a limited amount of
control over the future. That is where our focus should lie.
To dwell on the past is not only detrimental to us but
unfair to our spouses so it is something that we all vowed
not to do."

The next morning was Sunday. Brian's sermon was

from the letters of St. Paul. As Edward put it, "Something about husbands love your wives etc., etc." On the way home from church Edward stopped in the shop for a moment while Jennifer and Sarah went up the hill to make lunch. Edward walked up to the anvil, knelt down, and folded his hands on the top of it and spoke two words, "Thank you." He then stood up, and his foot kicked the broken handle that had fallen on the floor. He looked around for the hammerhead. Once he had found it, he worked out the piece of broken handle that was left in the head. He sat down with the two pieces in his hand, pushed them back together, and then took them apart. Laying one on top of the other in the shape of a cross, he nailed it high on the post just under the ring he had nailed up there in years past and went home.

About a month later Edward had occasion to go to Riverside to pick up some metal. While he was there, he looked up the doctors, and asked the intern who was just about to get his medical degree to come to the village and set up a practice. The doctor that he was interning with said that it is very expensive to set up a practice from scratch. Edward inquired as to how much it might cost. The doctor sized him up and finally said, "About 150 pounds." Then he continued with a long list of materials needed to set up a workable practice. The doctor said it would take this young man at least two or more years to amass such a sum before he could come to your village. Edward was very polite, and on his way out asked the young doctor if he would have lunch with him. During lunch, Edward made an offer to the young doctor. "If I were to give you 150 pounds, would you come to our village and start your practice?" The man was flabbergasted. He didn't think there was that much money in the entire village. He looked at Edward's questioning eye and began to speak, "I don't really have the experience.

I am only finishing my internship, and I feel as though…"
Edward cut him off by saying, "200 pounds." The young
man smiled and immediately said, "Yes." "When can you
start?" He thought for a moment and said, "I have one
more month of internship. I can be there by the fourth of
July." Edward stated, "I will have an office waiting for
you. I will be back next month with a large wagon to
deliver some chandeliers and pick up some rods. I will
have 200 pounds and room enough for any equipment you
might want me to carry back to the village. I will do this
for you under one condition, that is you tell no one about
the 200 pounds." They shook hands; the deal was closed.

A month later Edward returned. The young man told
him all the equipment that he wanted to make his office
the most modern and well-equipped office in the country
was 50 miles away, but he had no way of collecting it. It
was to be ready in a week, and he had to pick it up. A
week later Edward was back with O'Grady's log wagon,
ready to make the 50-mile trip.

A few weeks later the young doctor set up his
practice. And who was the very first patient to come see
the doctor--Noreen. Most of his calls over the next few
months were just routine calls. In the sixth month of his
practice, he delivered six babies all in the same month, two
of which were Jennifer's twins, Ed and Jen.

In the first summer of the twins' lives, the river
flooded. It rushed just over four feet of water down the
main street. Everyone in town made their way to the
plateau. They erected tents, and for three days watched
the water rush through the town. Edward gathered all the
men around the kitchen table. They all laid out plans on a
large piece of paper for building a levee from the far end of
Edward's property along the river all the way to O'Grady's

sawmill, which was up a hill on the other end of town. O'Grady had a canoe which he used to ferry people back and forth to their homes to retrieve things they needed. He also brought boards that Edward had requested to build a trough, which would be an extension of the water trough running by Jennifer's kitchen window. This trough would carry fresh mountain water down the hill to the edge of town where he planned to build a cistern to catch the water. All the men worked together, dug a trench, and laid the boards to make a trough which ran all the way down the hill to the edge of town, over 500 feet. The idea was to give everyone fresh water to wash the river muck out of their homes, and in the future would allow clean water for drinking and cooking which would be better than their many trips to the river. When the water subsided, everyone chipped in carrying water and washing every house one by one down the street until the entire village was washed clean.

There was much discussion about Edward's plan to build a levee. Edward insisted that even though it was probably a 100-year flood it would be worth the effort. He offered the dirt from his land to build a levee. At first many men worked on it, but it was taking so long and taking time away from their work. Construction began to slow until finally they only worked a few hours on the weekends. Edward persisted, and by the end of the second year the levee was complete. The rains came, and the river flooded about two feet above flood stage. The levee held. They named the day of the big flood, Levee Day. Every year after that they celebrated Levee Day.

The following summer the bears came one day. Eight bears came down from the mountain for no obvious reason late one night. They started raiding everyone's compost piles and then progressed to the garbage cans. When that didn't satisfy them enough, they broke windows and pushed in doors to get to the food in the houses. Everyone in town was shocked and amazed. The next day at a small town meeting some people thought that they would not come back, but Edward had lived in Indian villages and had experience with wild animals. He told them they always come back. So that night all the men positioned themselves with rifles and waited for the bears to return. They planned to attempt to fire at the bears simultaneously so they could get all of them before they ran off. The plan worked beautifully. The bears brazenly walked right down the street, seven large black bears with one straggling behind. When they got in range of all of the shooters, one man yelled fire and over 20 shots rang out, killing all but one bear. Edward skinned the bears in the way that he was taught by the Indians. He also insisted over some objections that they use every bit of the animal with no waste. He then showed them how it could be done. He had learned to tan many hides of animals when he lived with the Indians, and he did so with all seven bear skins. He then gave the skins to each of the men who had shot the bears.

The following year the traveling salesman came into town with his wagon. His clinking tin pots could be heard all over the village as he stopped in front of the general store. He always brought hundreds of articles to be sold in the store and things that people might have ordered on his last trip. He pulled up in front of the blacksmith's shop. His horse had a loose shoe. Edward took care of it for him. He then picked up several chandeliers as well as some wall mount candleholders and was on his way.

CHAPTER 5

"MULLIN, MULLIN!" yelled the traveling salesman when he was about three blocks away. Edward ran up the street to find out why he called. "Did something break? Are the chandeliers alright?" "Yes," the peddler answered, "I have forgotten to give you this letter," as he handed him a letter from his breast pocket. Edward was very surprised. He had never gotten a letter before. With a price on his head, he thought, if a letter can find me so can someone else. With much worry and trepidation he opened the letter. It had been sent two years ago on the same day that the eight women came down from his house. It read as follows:

"Dear Edward, I have sent this letter inside a letter to the magistrate in Boston. It is my hope that you have had some legal dealings such as buying property or selling something so that there is some record of you on file. I don't know if you will receive this letter or not, but I felt compelled to write to you. The Huguenot is dead. His daughter Anna has suspended the bounty on your head. When they received word that you had been seen on a pirate ship, he put a price on your head and annulled your wedding. Anna is married with three children. Aside from this news, my purpose for writing you is to ask you a favor. My son John and his daughter Priscilla sailed for America to a place called Plymouth. I have just received notice that they have come down with consumption and have died. It is probably too much to ask, but I am hoping that you might perhaps find it possible to see that their graves are properly marked. I hope this letter finds you well though it has been many years since we parted. Your brother, Charles"

Two months after the letter came Jennifer gave birth to a six-and-one-half pound baby girl, Priscilla. Then quite unexpectedly 15 minutes later, John was born. Edward waited until the twins were two years old and able to travel before he planned a vacation trip to the seashore. In early June, just when school was out, they packed up the family and headed for the seashore. He had rented a cabin on the shore, and the family spent two wonderful weeks swimming and playing in the sand. On the third week they took a side trip up to Plymouth. They found the vicar who pointed out the gravesites of John and Priscilla. There were no markings. They then found the local monument maker and arranged for proper markers for Edward's nephew and his daughter. Then he sat down and composed a letter to Charles, telling him that the graves were marked. While on vacation Edward told many, many stories about his time on the sea and how he loved it more than any other time in his life before he met Jennifer.

Over the next few years, Edward's oldest son, Little Ed, as they called him, became very interested in the chandelier-making business and began to take over that part of the business. The business really began to thrive because of Little Ed's creativity. He even made a chandelier out of a wagon wheel, which became extremely popular.

In the summertime, when the kids were out of school, Little Ed complained many times to his mother about his father telling stories to other children who hung around the blacksmith shop. "They're always in my way, and I have a hard time getting things done," Ed complained. His mother smiled and said, "You are not getting things done, because you're listening to the stories." Ed confessed, "I must say they are compelling, though I often wondered how much truth they hold." "Well," Jennifer replied, "You know his motto." "Yes, I do," and spontaneously and simultaneously they quoted together, "Never let the truth..." They both laughed.

It was the best of times as the years flew by. Edward enjoyed watching all of his children grow and spread their wings as they went off, each of them with their own goals in life. After the first summer they spent at the beach was such a success, it became an annual affair. Every time they went Edward's longing for the sea became stronger. The kids were grown, and only the twins, John and Priscilla, were left to go with them. It looked to Edward as though it may be the last time they would go to the beach as a family.

CHAPTER 6

"MULLIN, MULLIN, it's nice to see you again," Edward heard off in the distance as he and Jennifer were eating dinner in a restaurant on the coast. It was a friend of Brian's who was studying in a seminary up the coast. Brian had brought him into the blacksmith shop the summer before. While they were eating dinner, Jennifer overheard a conversation in the next booth. The man was complaining that it was necessary for him to travel over 100 miles around the bay to deliver his goods when it was only nine miles across the water. Over the winter Jennifer convinced Edward to explore the idea. He was able to procure several maps of the bay and planned his strategy. He would try to buy several acres on each of the points of land, one to the north and one to the south. He would have to build two piers and a house. He estimated the cost would be more than he had saved. This information was kept from Jennifer as he remembered he had a little over 150 pounds stashed away. He found it amazingly easy to buy the land and construct the piers. They would have to stay in a tent for the first summer until he could get enough money to build the house. He spent 150 pounds to buy a small ship that he converted into a ferry. It would hold two large wagons with horses or three to four small wagons. They were broke, but they were happy. The new business did very well. He made as many as four trips a day on a very good day, and on a bad day, only one. The unpredictable Atlantic always gave them a few days when they couldn't sail at all. He loved the sea so much he seldom failed to sail, no matter what the weather. No matter how difficult the sail, he seemed to love the challenge. Even better yet, he loved a captive audience to listen to his many tales. One couple that went back and forth several times were heard to say, "We love the ferry because of the stories the Captain tells."

After several years of ferrying back and forth and surviving the harsh winters the Atlantic provides, the old ferry began to show much wear and tear. He managed to save enough money to make a down payment on a new ship. Edward drew the plans for a super ferry that would hold as many as six wagons and 12 horses, with a deck below with a kitchen and dining area where Jennifer would cook and make some extra money. A few weeks after giving his money to the shipyard, he discovered that the shipyard was abandoned. The owner was nowhere to be found. Edward went to Boston and talked to O'Toole. The lawyer, unable to find the owner, managed to convince the court to sign the property over to Edward. Edward figured he was doomed. He had a ship that he spent more time bailing when sailing, an abandoned shipyard, and no money.

One day an old man came aboard with the shiniest, blackest surrey that Edward had ever seen. It was so highly polished that it reflected every light that touched it. Edward began to talk to the old man asking about the surrey. The old man told him that he and his son made the surreys, and he was delivering it to a rich man down the coast. As he listened to him talk, Edward had the feeling that he had seen him before. He asked, "Do I know you? You look familiar." The old man was hunched over with hundreds of wrinkles on his face. He turned his head to the side and looked up at Edward saying, "You look familiar to me. What is your name?" "Edward Mullin." The old man's eyebrows went up, and his eyes opened wide as he looked up at his face. "The navigator?" "Yes, I was a navigator. Wow, how do you know that?" The old man smiled and said nothing for a short while as Edward's curiosity grew. Finally he stated, "I sailed with you a few times in my younger days. That explains why you look familiar." "How many times did we sail together?"

Edward inquired. The old man was evasive and didn't
want to answer the question. Edward changed the subject
and told him the troubles he was having and that this was
probably one of the last voyages of this boat. The old man
was very curious about the problem so Edward explained
what had happened. When they arrived at the dock, the
man took his surrey and went on his way.

Two weeks later while Edward was bailing out the
boat at the dock he noticed one of those gleaming surreys
standing on the dock. His curiosity got the better of him,
and he walked out to investigate. He found a note on the
seat that said, "A gift for Edward Mullin for the times we
spent together." He searched all the way to the horizon to
see if he could see the old man. He then turned the note
over, and on the bottom in very tiny print, almost
impossible to read was one line, "Don't miss the secret
compartment under the seat. I have held it for you all
these years, Teague." He climbed in the surrey and felt
under the seat. There was nothing there. It was smooth
all the way across with the same amount of sheen under
the seat as everywhere else. He finally laid down and
looked at the underside. There was nothing there. He
then looked along the edge and found one little screw. He
took a coin from his pocket and turned the screw. Once it
was loose the entire bottom could slide towards the back
of the surrey. There was a slight indentation about an
eighth of an inch where he found ten 100-pound notes.
He push it back together, turned the screw, then took his
knife and sliced off the bottom of the note with the tiny
printing on it. He then called Jennifer to show the gift to
her. Jennifer loved the surrey, but she had only one
complaint. Every time she went around a corner she slid
across the seat into the side rail. Edward again had
trepidations about the money. When he got back to town,
he went to the blacksmith shop and hid it away as he had

done before. He worried that it was stolen money, and he didn't want to have any part of stolen money. His mind harkened back to the times when he saw people die because of money. He didn't feel that he wanted to build his life on blood money. On the other hand, Teague obviously felt that he had stolen time from him and wanted to pay him back for it. Then again this could be money that he made legitimately, as unlikely as that might be. It put him in the same dilemma that he was in before, lying to Jennifer when he promised he would not. He thought and thought, searching for a solution to this problem. He was sure that this story, or should I say lie, would have to be every color that exists to be plausible.

He decided to go a few weeks early ahead of Jennifer to make sure that his ferry could make another year. While he was there, he went to the local banker and asked to borrow a hundred pounds against the land and boatyard. While talking to the banker, he told him about the boatyard. He asked if he knew anyone who would be interested in buying it. The banker said no, but he knew the men who worked in the yard were still looking for work. Edward asked for their names and addresses, then went around and looked them up. He found the head foreman who was in charge of the boatyard in the past and was left high and dry by his former owner. He discussed with him the possibility of opening the yard again and building a ferry, perhaps two, then asked if he was interested. Timothy O'Rourke took over the day-to-day operations and hired the men to begin construction within a week for Edward's super ferry. When the first ferry was only half complete, they laid the keel for the second.

Meanwhile, Edward built a building by the dock, the downstairs of which was a restaurant where people could wait for the ferry. The upstairs was a two-bedroom apartment where they lived. Timothy talked Edward into hiring a salesman who would go out and find people to buy ships. The old ferry got so bad he had to hire a bailing boy just to keep her afloat. The men worked through the summer and into the winter building the two ferries. Both ferries were ready at the beginning of the following summer. Edward tried to convince his son John to become a sailor and took him along to teach him how to sail, but he spent most of his time hanging over the rail losing his lunch. He seemed to have no interest at all. John spent a lot of time in the kitchen with Jennifer learning to cook. Edward set him up in the restaurant as a chef.

Then one day, one of Teague's men showed up on the ferry and told Edward that Teague had died. Edward asked him if there were other men from the crew in the area. He said yes, and some of them had taken care of their money and have gone legit. Others were broke. Edward told them he was looking for another captain and crew for his other ferries. Within a few days seven men showed up, all of them with more experience on the sea than anyone else in the world. He had a meeting with them. The first words from his mouth were, "You will kill no one. You will steal from no one. You will make no solicitations. If you do, I will kill you and nail your ears to the main mast." Edward knew that Teague was taking care of these guys even though they had squandered their money. He thought that Teague would have wanted him to use some of this money to take care of them. As far as he knew over the next few years, they had kept their promise of no killing, no stealing, or cavorting. By this time they were all in their 60s and unwilling to lose their ears.

In the spring of the fourth year Edward announced to Jennifer that he had paid back the bank with interest.

On one of the ferry crossings a passenger was belligerent. He was unhappy with the service, unhappy with the food, and yelling at one of the men for giving oats to his horse. He grabbed the sailor who had given the oats, smashing him against the wall and shoving him back behind the horse. The old sailor's pirate blood began to boil, but he managed to contain himself enough to go to Edward and asked, "Let me kill that son of a bitch. We can throw him over the side, and no one will miss him." Edward replied, "Let me handle it." Edward went to the man who immediately began yelling at him about the poor service, the oats, the sailor, etc. After the man calmed down, Edward talked to him for a while, and the man began to reveal why he was so upset. He was in debt, losing his business and possibly his wife because of it. He did not know what to do. Edward listened to his story, and when they docked, he called the man over and shook his hand. Edward had folded up a 100-pound note and held it in his palm when he shook his hand. He looked up at Edward in questioning disbelief. Edward said, "I too was in need, and someone helped me. I don't want you to pay me back. Sometime in the future you may run across someone who needs help, and you can pass it along." The man looked up at him smiling and promised, "I will."

When winter came up, they put the boats in dry dock and headed back to the village to spend the winter months. That summer the village became large enough to be incorporated as a town. As they came into the village, there was a sign that said, "Welcome to Edwardsville." Edward couldn't believe it. He almost floated into town. Jennifer got out at the general store to pick up food for the evening meal. That night at the dinner table he was bragging on the idea that the town liked him so much that they name it after him. Jennifer let him gloat for a while until he said he was going down to the tavern. She stopped him before he left and told him that the town was not named after him. It was named after Glenn Quincy Edwards, who was the first settler in the area. As a matter of fact, the old blacksmith was a son of Quincy Edwards.

Instead of going to the tavern he went down to the blacksmith shop to visit his son. He was out front shoeing a horse so Edward went inside. He was thinking about his disappointment, which prompted him to look up at the post where the ring and the broken handle cross were nailed. He noticed below the cross was a spoon and below that was a piece of yarn, both of which were nailed in the same manner. Even though curiosity was burning a hole in

his brain, he decided not to inquire. He thought, "It is nice to know that I'm not the only person who needs a reminder now and then."

In the spring when they put the ferry back in the water and started the service once more, four paddy wagons filled with policemen came on board to be transported across. Edward found himself without a crew and managed with the help of a couple of passengers to get the ferry underway. While talking to the Chief of Police, he was told that they were out looking for pirates. There was a rumor that there were pirates in the area. The wind was steady so Edward tied off the wheel and began to search the ship for his crew. He looked over the back rail, and one of them was sitting on the ledge behind the rail. He grabbed him by the hair and pulled them up. He told him to take the wheel and not to worry. He then found the others, and he had them meet him by the wheel. They all made their way to the wheel without letting anyone see their faces. Edward told them that they were looking for a ship somewhere up the coast, not to worry, and to get back to work.

There were several companies that shipped their goods up and down the coast in very large wagons. These wagons were too large for the ferry so Edward made a deal with them to leave their boxes on the dock, and he would ship them to the other side where they could be picked up by teamsters on the other pier and carried on. The teamsters liked the arrangement, because they could be home at night instead of making the long trek all the way up to New York, spending the night, and coming back. The shipping was taking up much of the space on each crossing so Edward decided to build another ferry just for shipping.

One day when the shipping ferry was a few weeks from completion, Edward was wondering about how he was going to man the new ferry. One afternoon Edward's ferry had only shipping crates and no passengers. He set sail to do his normal crossing. About half way, as in every crossing, they began to pass his other ferry, which had passengers in the galley who were singing and having a grand time. The sailors signaled to Edward to come alongside, because they had found a wallet with money in it. They gave the wallet to Edward to take back to the ferry dock they had just come from. As he tied up alongside, another ship seemed to come from nowhere. Edward instructed his sailors to arm themselves with steak knives from the kitchen, just in case there might be a problem. The men from the unknown ship boarded the ferry that had passengers. Edward went down to close the door so the passengers wouldn't hear anything that might happen. Just as the ship came alongside, two men swung across on ropes and jumped down toward the deck only to be met by a steak knife in their bellies. The ship came in closer, and the crew dropped a gangplank across between the two ships. Four men rushed on board. Edward's crews were hiding along the rail. As the men came down the gangplank, they pulled them off and slit their throats. All of this happened within the space of a minute. When Edward came back up from closing the door, he discovered the situation with six dead pirates. There were still four men on the pirate ship, who after seeing what happened, stood at the head of the gangplank with their hands in the air. Edward jumped across to the other ferry while one of his men asked, "Should I slit their throats?" "No!" Edward yelled, "What did I tell you about killing?" The sailor looked at him in disgust, "It was a raiding party. They came to kill us." Edward looked at the four men and asked, "Are you pirates?" The four men rolled her eyes and replied, "No, we are just a friendly passerby." Edward shook his head and said, "Pirates." One sailor said, "Can I kill him now?" "NO, let me talk to them. Meanwhile put these bodies back on the ship, rig it for full sail pointed out to sea, and tie the wheel down. Then row back here in that little dinghy hanging on the back." Edward sat down with the four men and made a deal. He told them, "I need a crew for my new ferry. If you want a chance at a new life, this is your opportunity. What I have just told you is your option number one. Your option number two is to have your throats slit and thrown in the sea. Which is it, gentlemen?" These four men were the ones who lagged behind when the boarding happened so Edward believed that they weren't the sharpest tools in the shed. As time went on, his theory proved to be correct. They proved to be useful raising sails and loading boxes but for little else. When his men rode back in the very small dinghy, it was drawing water within four inches of the gunwales. The men had found a strongbox and brought it back with them. At the end of the day, they all met in the kitchen of the restaurant and sat with the strongbox on the table. Edward told them that whatever was in the box would be divided among them under one condition, that they would not quit their jobs. He did not want to have a share. When they opened the box, they found gold coins, 1200 pounds in cash, some promissory notes, and then a map that showed the location of a buried treasure. The old pirate spirit bubbled up in nearly all the men at the thought of a buried treasure. Edward then closed the treasure chest and noted to everyone that there was sand stuck in all the little nooks and crannies. He pointed out that the map was leading them to this very box. This was the treasure once buried. He also asked them an interesting question, "When did you ever bury a treasure?" Edward put the dinghy out in front of the restaurant, filled with it dirt and made it into a planter. He stuck a post in the middle of it, and put a skull and crossbones flag on top of the post.

Inside the restaurant he displayed the treasure chest and the map on the wall. He hung a sign over the front door that read, "The Jolly Roger."

It was a bright sunny morning with the nor'easter coming in about seven knots, a perfect day for sailing. Edward couldn't wait to shove off and feel the wind in his face. They boarded fours teams of horses and wagons loaded with supplies for the shops in the North. They sailed about an hour when they noticed far out on the horizon an ominous black cloud. It had a few lightning flashes, but it appeared to be moving out to sea so Edward thought nothing of it. They sailed on for about a mile or so. Jennifer came up with some blueberry muffins she had made in the kitchen. She remarked how beautiful the day was before she went below. Edward was telling one of his stories to the passengers when all of a sudden one of them pointed out to sea. When Edward looked, he saw an enormous wave. He immediately turned the bow toward the wave in an attempt to ride over it, but he only turned the ferry about 45°degrees to the wave when it lifted the ferry up a good 30 feet and broke over the top, sending the ferry upside down to the bottom amidst the sound a passenger yelling, "MULLIN!"

Edward Mullin, Jennifer Mullin die in tidal wave

Edward, 84, born in Ireland, and Jennifer, 79, born in Edwardsville, passed away on Aug. 8, 1710. They are survived by five of their children: Sarah, Ed, Jen, Priscilla, and John. Edward was a navigator, captured by pirates, lived with Indians, was a blacksmith, owned and operated a ferry line. Jennifer was a schoolteacher for 40 years before she worked on the ferry with her husband for 17 years prior to the accident.

174

Authors Note

The newspaper clipping was found in my father's genealogy research papers when he passed away. I filled in the blanks and created this story about how Edward Mullin brought the Mullin family name to America.

176

Acknowledgement

I would like to thank my wife, Rhonda, for her
extraordinary work as proofreader, fact checker,
researcher, and in-house agent.

Thanks for being my computer guru who guides me
through the computer minefield. Without her continuing
efforts to see that this book is finished,
it would have never have seen the white of page.

178

About the Author

John Mullin is the author of three books (Piccolo Conscript, ABC'z, and MULLIN), which he has both written and illustrated. He holds two degrees, a BFA and MFA. He has enjoyed operating his own design studio for over 35 years. He is married, a father of three, and currently lives in Northwest Indiana.